Marie Vere Farrington

Fra Lippo Lippi

Marie Vere Farrington

Fra Lippo Lippi

ISBN/EAN: 9783337049409

Printed in Europe, USA, Canada, Australia, Japan

Cover: Foto ©Andreas Hilbeck / pixelio.de

More available books at **www.hansebooks.com**

FRA LIPPO LIPPI

A ROMANCE

BY

MARGARET VERE FARRINGTON

AUTHOR OF "TALES OF KING ARTHUR AND HIS KNIGHTS OF
THE ROUND TABLE"

WITH FOURTEEN PHOTOGRAVURE ILLUSTRATIONS

G. P. PUTNAM'S SONS

NEW YORK   LONDON
27 WEST TWENTY-THIRD ST.   27 KING WILLIAM ST., STRAND

The Knickerbocker Press

1890

TO
W. F. L.

CONTENTS.

ILLUSTRATIONS.

Questi m' ha fatto men amare Dio
   Ch' i' non devea, e men curar me stesso :
   Per una donna ho messo
   Egualmente in non cale ogni pensiero.
     .   .   .   .   .

   Misero ! a che quel chiaro ingegno altero
   E l' altre doti a me date del Cielo ?

      —PETRARCH, Canz. vii. *(In Morte di Laura.)*

FRA LIPPO LIPPI.

I.

HEN the Abbess of Santa Margharita at last consented to have the convent chapel frescoed, three things perplexed her. To be sure Father Antonio, as well as the holy priests from Santa Maria del Fiore, had always urged the painting. They had often said when they came to mass at Prato, that such sombre naves, such bare walls, and such rude mouldings were contrary to the true spirit of worship. Yet the Abbess would question the wisdom of that advice, to which, nevertheless, she felt obliged to yield. Not that she objected to seeing the martyrdoms of the saints or the Passion of our Lord ever depicted before her, but she decidedly rebelled against having the dim, sacred chapel, where she prostrated herself in penance and prayer, glow with life and color,—indeed flame with any light other than that from the taper on the altar.

What colorist could ever reproduce the portrait of the Blessed Virgin as painted by St. Luke? It was imaged in the Abbess' heart as the very impersonation of beauty, simple gentleness, humility, sanctified purity, maternal love, and sublime heroism. Her very soul exclaimed against the profaneness which represented the peerless mother of Christ under the features of some too well known duchess, unveiled, decked in glittering robes as if to allure by earthly loveliness.

Were not the very Holy of Holies in Florence turned into mere picture-galleries, and for the most part painted by unworthy hands,—only now and then a monk like gentle Fra Angelico weeping and praying as he portrayed the sorrows of Christ and the saints! The Abbess had not caught the artistic spirit which had budded and blossomed in Florence —Florence! how she hated that magnificent, passionate city! She shuddered as she thought it was just a hundred years ago since Prato, finally exhausted by intrigues, had actually given up its liberty and had been ground in the dust by the despots of the conquering city; how the old houses had declined and new ones had risen to power. With the decline of the aristocracy in Florence, their adherents in neighboring cities had gone down too; when the fortunes of the imperial party had suddenly changed, the Guazziolitri, her family, loyal supporters of the Popes in all their disputes and discords and wars, were driven from their homes, their fortunes confiscated, their palaces in possession of the invaders.

What if there was a little calm in that fickle city, tumult might break out at any time; what if beautiful churches had risen through the riches of the feudal nobles and

powerful guilds, what if the arts did flourish,
—was it in this way these feasting, dancing,
corrupt followers of the Medici ruffians expected to save their souls from purgatory?
The Abbess reverently crossed herself as she
thought of the moral baseness of the poli-
ticians who made their hypocritical religion a
tool of the state.

Yes; let them build their gorgeous palaces
and cathedrals, and fill them with carvings
and statues and pictures, but the convent of
Santa Margharita, ah,—would that it could
be in its chaste simplicity, as a veiléd bride
ready for the heavenly bridegroom, instead of
a conscious woman in splendid apparel.

As for the painting,—first there would be
the confusion in the worship consequent to
the staging, and certain delay in decoration.
In the second place, the convent rules must
be more rigidly enforced. Last of all, the
Bishop of Santa Maria had engaged Fra
Filippo Lippi to paint the Madonna over the
high altar, and the Abbess had a premonition
of evil.

Whatever interfered with the worship naturally perplexed the Abbess, for the convent
buildings were not large, and some special
arrangement must be made with the workmen
for the vacancy of the chapel during mass.
But the difficulty was that there would be the
longer delay in frescoing because of this constant interruption.

To enforce the church rules perplexed the
Abbess still more since the convent stood on a
hill just outside the town, and greater liberty
was allowed the novices and nuns than at
Florence. The garden, shut within walls,
was far from the clamor of the streets, and at
such a distance the noises of the city were
carried over the tree-tops, or lost and indistin-
guishable in the rustling leaves.

It was the habit of the nuns to leave the
convent court-yard with its plashing fountain
and heavy, perfumed air, for the grass-grown
terrace or the cool orchard,—the broader out-
of-doors world of theirs. Here they could see
more blue sky, and look below the hill-slope
to the sunlit, misty valley, where the little

sparkling river flowed lazily to the Arno. It
was so calm and restful here above the blos-
soming vineyards, with only the sweet clang-
ing of the bell in its open tower to break the
silence ; but with the workmen and painters,—
monks though they were,—the Abbess decided
that whatever sunlight and air the nuns took
during the next few weeks must be from the
low windows of their rooms. Only that very
day the Abbess had seen Sister Theresa, who
recently had been rescued from a union with
the young dissolute Duke of Verona, and who
had lately taken vows of allegiance to only a
celestial spouse,—yet, in spite of all this, she
had seen her look long and earnestly at an
illuminated text in which was a head of Saint
Augustine. The Abbess could not deny that
it was a handsome head, and she fancied that
Lippo Lippi had one very much resembling it.

Yes, it would be necessary to increase the
days of fasting and hours of penance, for, of
all things most perplexing, Lippi was a Carmelite monk. Not that she knew very much
about him, or the Church of the Carmine, but

it was not of the seraphic order of St. Francis
under which the convent of Santa Margharita
was founded. And as for Lippi, was it not
enough that the hot-headed Florentines were
singing his praises, and that Cosmo de Medici
was his patron?

Not many weeks before she had lingered for
a few moments in the doorway of Santo Stefano. Lippi was then frescoing the choir of
the Cathedral, but she had not even been in to
see it. She was waiting for one of the Sisters
to join her, when she overheard there some
young monks enthusiastically praising the
work of the brilliant Carmelite artist. She
knew then, as well as after that, when the
Bishop came to the convent to urge the
painting, she would not like Fra Lippi.

Was it the law of contradiction? It might
be. Any way, this was the beginning of her
prejudice. Yet now she almost wished that
she had just looked into the Cathedral. It
need not appear that she had come to see the
fresco, for she often went in the choir to look
through the railing into the chapel where that

most sacred relic, the Cintola of the Virgin
was kept. She began to finger her rosary a
little uneasily as she remembered that she had
sometimes lingered as long in looking at that
exquisite gate designed by Ghiberti as she had
in worshipping the Cintola, or saying prayers
for Michael Dogomari, who, through his marriage with the fair daughter of a Greek priest
at Jerusalem, had brought the blessed treasure to Prato. How näively Agnolo Gaddi
had told that story with his brush and his
colors. She was sure she should not like
Lippi's painting as well as those old frescos
in the chapel, for the reason that Masaccio,
his master, had turned his back on the world
of ecstatics, on mystical Fra Angelico, who
painted only angels beheld in visions. Masaccio painted men and women about him, the
flesh and blood of Florence. She knew that
Lippi had abandoned himself with recklessness from the ideal to the real.

Ah! who indeed should adorn the ceiling
of Santa Margharita, now that the Angel
Painter was dead! The Abbess sighed as she

thought how she had waited all these years for Fra Angelico to portray for the nuns the truths of the invisible world. Only seven years ago he had been brought to Prato to fresco the greater chapel of Santo Stefano, but suddenly left the next day without a word to the disappointed rectors of the commune. What Madonnas of ineffable sweetness and purity would have looked down upon the sad penitents if he had painted them! The Abbess felt that there must be grave and powerful reasons that prompted him to leave Prato, and from that day she had thought it impious to consider decorating cathedral or convent in that unhappy city.

The holy fathers had suggested Benozzi Gozzoli;—yes, he was a pupil of the saintly Frate, yet she felt once when she had seen his vintage gatherers and festal troops of cavaliers, his marriage dances of youths and maidens, that he had not followed his master in his embodied ecstasies, nor could she agree with the priests in thinking that, by the grace of the Virgin, a holy mind had been given him with which he looked upon the earthly beauty of men and women about him, that he might spiritualize it. Indeed, Lippi himself could not seem more smitten by the beauty of the natural world.

What saints and Madonnas were taking the place of Cimabue's and Giotto's celestial beings! They, whether bearing the lily or the sword, the palm or the crown, were beings full of mystery, of power, of dignity ; the tranquillity of the ethereal regions bespoke itself in the peacefully folded hands and repose of spirit, and brought a message to the restless flaunting Florentines.

But if the holy fathers insisted, they should bring to the convent some one whose painting would breathe the same gentle, devotional spirit of the mystical painters.

.   .   .   .

The Bishop of Santa Maria was surprised to find the Abbess so indifferent about the Madonna fresco, when he came to see her after sending word about Fra Lippi. He had supposed the mere fact that Lippi was to

Madonna della Stella

Fra Angelico

be the artist would be enough to insure enthusiasm, and he only made matters worse by
his talk with the Abbess.

"You know what he has done already in
Florence," he said.

The Abbess gravely bowed her head, and
said in a low tone: "May the Holy Mother
save us!"

II.

HE convent of Santa Margharita was built, after the manner of convents of the thirteenth century, in a hollow square. It was of gray stone, simple, harmonious, with little rich carving or ornamentation. The Byzantine arches of the cloistered walk were its chief beauty, but it was necessary to open the heavy wooden gate to see them as well as the court-yard, with its orange-trees and grape-vines, its waving rose-bushes, or to smell the sweet breath of the violets which encircled the fountain. Passing through an arched opening in the southern corner of the court, a walk led to the vegetable and herb garden, and the orchard beyond. This was shut in by a high wall, except on one side, where a long parapet of dusky tiles left open the beautiful view of the Val d'Arno.

Here, under the fruit-laden boughs in the orchard, wooden crosses marked the resting-places of nuns who had lived and died in the convent. In a corner, where the ilex foliage was thickest, one cross stood apart from the others; the dark green branches shadowed it, and wandering ivy vines clambered up and wound around the arms, nearly concealing letters carved in the wood,—the name of the first Abbess, Sister Margharita.

It was just about two hundred years before, that there lived in Prato a knight who had one beautiful daughter. This knight was from a most noble family, and one of the first to band a company of young nobles to support Manfred and his eight hundred knights, in defiance of the Guelphs,—of the tyranny of Pope Alexander IV.

Through the dreary, exciting years of Michael Gonfali's absence, the child blossomed into a woman with black hair and languorous eyes. Michael had evidently forgotten the flight of years, for it surprised him to find Lucia no longer a child,—but he was proud of the grace of his daughter. It discomforted him to think that he had brought home that blonde-haired Saxon, Rudolph, who came with Manfred's men—that sword-wound would have healed as quickly in Naples as in Prato.

There was little calm in Tuscany, even though peace had been formally declared and Manfred crowned. After victories, old disputes awakened within the very walls of the town, and Michael Gonfali had plenty to do in quelling neighborly quarrels.

The pain in Saxon Rudolph's arm kept him from riding or walking around the city, and he spent most of his time in the courtyard; his favorite seat was under the arcades, where Lucia came to listen, for hours at a time, to war tales. Manfred thought that if, in the course of human events, wounds heal, certainly the gash in Rudolph's arm had been given plenty of time at the house of Michael

Gonfali; then, too, he missed his favorite and called him to the land of the olives. With passionate kisses and murmurs of love, Rudolph held Lucia in his arms; she clung weeping about his neck, begging him to stay.

An hour later, sad-eyed and heavy-hearted, she looked out of the window and saw the end of a blue velvet mantle floating in the wind, the nodding of plumes, the flash of a sword-hilt,—then she covered her ears with her hands that she might not hear the sound of the horse's hoofs die away in the distance.

Lucia never saw her blue-eyed, fair-skinned Saxon knight again. Very possibly he found the women of Naples more beautiful. At any rate the skies were purpler, the air more dreamy, the wine better,—and it was vastly pleasanter to play cavalier in the king's court than to be fighting these passionate Tuscan rebels. The days made weeks, and the weeks made months, Lucia scarcely noticing the change, until one night she found herself thrust out of the palace, and the gates shut against her. She wandered about the streets until finally

exhausted, then sank before the door of an old
house on the hill-slope just outside the city.

She knew no more until she awoke and
found a babe nestling in her arms. It was on
that very day Manfred fought his last battle;
victory had seemed almost his—and Rudolph,
with his sword raised high, shouting to the
men, was struck down by the very hand that
slew the king.   When the stars came out that
night, king and knight lay side by side on the
battle-field of Benevento.

In the change of fortunes the Guelphs were
at the head of government.   The family of
Michael Gonfali were again excommunicated
by Urban IV.   A small part of his fortune in
some way came to Lucia, with the provision
that she should use it for the Church.   So she
founded a convent and named it for Margaret,
the patron saint of repentant Magdalens.
The convent became a shelter for the betrayed, deserted women of Tuscany, whom
other things than war had robbed of their
homes and lovers.

After the death of Lucia (who had taken

the name of Sister Margharita), the child, who had grown up in the convent, utterly ignorant of the sins and sorrows of the real world, was made abbess.

So the years went by, until nearly two centuries had passed, and five more crosses were added to the first one placed in the orchard. Then one of the nuns, who had taken the name of the saint in whose honor the convent was founded, was made abbess. Sister Margharita had lived in the convent since she was a maiden of only fifteen years. Even in so sunny a land as Italy, the Abbess' girlhood had been full of shadow.

Among the hundreds of noble families exiled was that of her father. She remembered how she, when but a mere child, was taken on a long journey—how they had to leave their beautiful home and go to a land of strangers. One day her father was killed, then her mother died,—then some one brought her to Florence, and she lived with an old relative who never allowed her any

2

liberty for fear the Medici would find out
that a daughter of the banished Guazziolitri
was in that city.

De Medici! How she hated that name!
It meant to her all that was cruel and corrupt. Were they not from a family neither
noble nor distinguished? Had not Salvestro
and Ciompi united the lowest classes for the
sake of destroying the nobles? Her heart
thrilled at the deeds of her ancestors from
the time the Hohenstaufens ruled the world.

And now they were dead, banished by
these despots, while she, in the course of
years, had found refuge in a convent and
become its abbess.

She thought of the morning, long years
ago, when she started out with Monna Maria
to go to market; how she strayed from her
aunt's side, and wandered to the Duomo and
stood in front of it watching the men as they
worked on the great cupola.

The whole Piazza was noisy with the rush
and roar of busy life, and brilliant with the
mass of glitter of the ducal cavalcade coming

that way. She stood looking at the gold-embroidered mantles, the beautiful faces, the jewelled hands, the flash of dagger-hilts, when suddenly some one shouted and seized her by her shoulder. She saw a white horse with its princely rider dashing towards her—she started to run out of the way, but stumbled against a stone and fell. When she opened her eyes she saw the white horse quietly standing near, while its rider was bending over her binding a strip of silk about her bruised wrist. Then the bewildering cortege swept by. She never forgot that face. To her it was all that was beautiful and princely, with its soft waving hair, tender eyes, and smiling mouth. She used to long to run away again and watch in the squares and piazzas for a return of the ducal party (even though she still hated them for the bitter wrongs to her father), for the sight of a white horse with its youthful rider.

In so sunny a land she soon grew to be a maiden, but the face of her prince had not faded away with other childish dreams.

One day she was sitting on a grass-grown terrace near her aunt's little villa, when, by the flourish of trumpets, the flash of swords, the gay trappings of the horses, the glittering jewels and colors, she knew a party of nobles was coming that way. The almond bushes concealed her, but peering out through the leaves, she saw a youth more princely than the rest, mounted on a snow-white horse. Hours go quickly when one sits dreaming, and it seemed but a few moments before she saw a single horseman returning, leading his steed which limped as if from a sprain. He guided it to the terrace as if to rest in the shade, when suddenly a maiden as beautiful as a wood-nymph sprang from the tree, it seemed to him, and as quickly disappeared behind the sheltering wall opposite. She had dropped her flowers; he picked up one of the blossoms, put it in his doublet, and slowly rode back to the palace. In those fair days it often happened that the maid sat by the almond bush, and Francesco rode that way and rested in the shade. One dreadful day Monna Maria came there too.

The Abbess Maigharita

After that the maiden never left the court-
yard alone, and though Francesco rode that
way and looked for a pair of violet eyes, he
never saw them. Monna Maria had a long
talk at the confessional with Fra Giovanni—
and the next day the pretty maid, pale from
weeping, found herself in the convent of
Santa Margharita. So she entered upon the
dark and dismal paths of penance, and faithfully prayed that, for the sake of family
wrongs, the love for a Florentine noble might
be rooted from her heart ; that every memory of those dark eyes (which seemed to look
out of the convent recesses), and every accent
of the low voice (which she even now hears
in murmurs), should be forgotten. Ah, that
she, a Guazziolitri, should be guilty of so
passionate a love for one of the foes of her
house ! The pain, the penance, wore upon
her ; the roundness and red bloom of her
cheek faded ; the violet eyes lost their dreamy
light, and became deep and sad.

The years dragged by. Then came the
wretched war between Florence and Milan,
and Francesco mounted his horse and rode

off to fight for his beloved city. Meanwhile
the years of girlhood were left far behind,
and the sad woman, by her beautiful life, was
chosen abbess.

One night, just ten years ago, she was in
Florence. It was during Holy Week, and
long after midnight she was prostrated before
the crucifix, when she heard the Dominican
Brothers of the San Marco chanting. She
was strangely moved by a voice she distinguished from the others, and looking out of
the window, saw by the flare of the torches
one who she knew, by his bearing, was Francesco. Stunned, she watched the monks as
they passed in their black-and-white robes.

So he, too, had laid down name and fame,
and taken up the cross and cowl. His head
had lost its proud poise, and in the flare of
the torch she had seen that the old tender
love-light had burned out of his eyes, and his
face was seared and drawn by fierce sorrows.

The Abbess returned to Prato early the
next morning. She had not been to Florence
since that day.

III.

HE Bishop of Santa Maria had made all necessary arrangements for Lippi to begin the painting. He was a little touched when he saw the sad light in the Abbess' eyes ; he had always—despite his vows of renunciation of women— thought her eyes very beautiful. When the long dark lashes fell curling over them, they seemed to him like spring violets hiding in shadow. Perhaps if he had not taken so deep a vow he would have held the Abbess' hand and looked longer into the dark-blue depths of her eyes—as he did the morning, so many years ago, when she was brought to the confessional. Even then, she

23

was a beautiful child-woman, and knowing
her history so well, there had always been a
tender place for her in his heart.

Before this the Bishop had never opposed
the Abbess Margharita ; but now—now—she
had been a woman for many years, and surely
these years of service and prayer must have
so far softened her sorrows that she had forgotten the handsome young knight, Francesco.
Why, he himself had buried the heartaches of
youth long ago, and grown stout and com-
fortable in the monastery.

The climate of Italy was too soft to make
the warfare of its Christian soldiers too grave,
too austere ; the dreamy mists and soothing
winds must have lulled the Abbess' disappointment, even if they had not driven them quite
away.

Yes ; he was truly grieved to see that the
Abbess did not raise her eyes from that old
statue of St. Margaret standing there in the
cloister. It made him all the more uncomfortable to look at that barbarously crude
carving of the thirteenth century. He grew

impatient as he thought of the Abbess' unwillingness to have the convent decorated.
Why, he would like all the ceiling under the
arcades painted blue, and spangled with stars.
Then, too, there should be scenes from the
life of the Virgin on the side walls,—but after
Lippi had finished his beautiful fresco—then,
ah! then, he knew the Abbess would not rest
until the whole interior glowed with colors
from his magic brush.

A happy thought just then came to the
holy father,—perhaps the Abbess had a choice
as to what scene from the life of the blessed
Virgin Lippi should portray.

The Abbess was diverted. There was a
scene so closely relating to a miracle in which
Prato was concerned, that she gratefully smiled
at the Bishop and nodded her head. And so
the matter was settled.

Three days later, the Abbess, looking from
her window, saw a Carmelite monk, with three
attendants, enter the convent court. It was
but an hour after sunrise, and she had just

returned from early mass in the chapel. She knew that the monk must be Lippi, and the men the carpenters to prepare the staging. She watched them as they crossed the hollow square towards the chapel entrance, for her room was opposite the row of arcades which extended from the court door, and she could see the men pass under the arches. Fra Lippi was the tallest of the four, and although she had not been able to see his face as she looked down into the court, there was an air of independence in his general bearing which bespoke the genius which commanded so much admiration in Florence.

The men seemed to follow him naturally. She noticed one of them step forward and speak a few words to him—apparently to suggest that yonder door was that of the chapel—and then resume his place a little behind Lippi.

When the Abbess descended to the chapel, an hour after, she found the carpenters at work building a rude staging above the altar, while Lippi gave them directions. He was standing with his back toward her as she entered, and it was not till she had walked almost the entire length of the nave that he seemed to be aware of her approach. As he turned toward her, she was impressed again by his tall figure—and now she saw what she could not from her window.

It was a handsome face—and yet the difficulty was to know just where the power lay. There was something so far from self-consciousness in it, that it attracted the Abbess.

"I see," she began, as if almost at a loss what to say, "that you are at work already, Fra Lippi."

"Yes, according to the Bishop's orders. With the staging completed, I shall soon be painting," he replied, looking questioningly into the Abbess' face.

"And how long before all is done?"

"I cannot tell. It is more difficult to paint sometimes than at other. I shall reserve the Madonna for the last. It may be that under the inspiration of this holy place I shall be more successful in hastening the work than elsewhere."

There was something almost facetious in this remark, but the Abbess did not notice it. Lippi began calling her attention to the bare walls and general dreariness of the chapel, suggesting the various improvements that might be made. He described to her briefly some of the painting he had done in chapels, and the general effect of the predella, lunette, and Madonna above the high altar. These of course were to be his special paintings— and then the moulding and walls might be made to harmonize. The chapel would be beautified wonderfully. "Yet the changes would not interfere with her love for the holy place," added Lippi adroitly, as he saw the Abbess glance about half-hesitatingly. "She would love it all the more," he said reassuringly. And the Abbess looked convinced.

All these suggestions were made by Lippi with a delicate deference which unconsciously appealed to the Abbess. Before she knew it, the interest which the Carmelite artist had excited in her by his enthusiasm and true artistic taste, joined with his evident forgetfulness of self in the identification of himself so early with the work, made heavy inroads upon the Abbess' prejudice so apparent in her conversation with the Bishop.

In fact, she remained longer in the chapel with Fra Lippi than she could believe. When returning to her room she found that the hour-glass had emptied itself in her absence. She had even been drawn into making sugges-tions, and all these were accepted or modified by Lippi with a quiet politeness and respect which she liked. These were the things that she remembered most frequently when her thoughts turned occasionally during the day to the chapel.

The Abbess grew daily surprised at the amount of interest she took in the work. Every morning she went to the chapel and quietly watched the painting. The weeks went on. Lippi had worked faithfully. The lunette, with its frame of arabesques, figures, and heads, was finished. *The Adoration, The Dedication in the Temple, The Murder of the Innocents* of the predella, were painted with masterful touches. The only thing that troubled the Abbess was the difficulty Fra

Lippi found in painting the face of the Holy
Virgin.   He would paint, then hesitate, then
destroy,—and she felt sure there was need of
fasting and penance.

As the days went on she timidly broached
the subject of night prayers that the blessed
Mother might reveal herself to him in vision,
as she did to the Angel Painter.

Fra Lippi's face was turned from her, so she
did not see the smile that came to his lips and
eyes—if she had it would have only strength-
ened her belief that he made life a far too
merry-go-lucky thing.   She often had an un-
easy feeling that his face was too bright and
his smile too careless.   She wondered what
the new novice just come to Santa Margharita's meant when she whispered to Lucrezia
Buti that " Lippi would not have to be fastened in here—there were more pretty eyes in
the convent than there were in the empty
chapel of Cosmo de Medici."   She would carefully watch that young girl, for it was plain to
see that she belonged to the thoughtless, latter-day Florentines.

IV.

IFE was no mere existence with Lippi. He loved light and air and mirth. To be in the great, real world, to feel its sunshine, its joy, its freedom, to chafe under the conventional, to break away and know the fascination of recklessness—this to him was life. It had always been so. That morning when his aunt taking him by the hand had led him, a boy of eight years, to the Carmine, he had known her real reason, but she told the monks she must give him into their charge because of her poverty. How often he had disobeyed her in running away at early morning down the bye street, Ardiglion, to be gone all day,

31

joining the other boys and leading on to what
they often planned but did not dare.

Once—it was only a few weeks before—two
of the monks of the Carmine had passed the
group at play, and it was Filippo who, running
behind, mischievously pulled the cloak of the
taller, who turned as if to catch the little rogue.
The other monk smiled as he looked back at
the boy,—he was such a picturesque little fel-
low with his loose shirt showing a round throat
almost as brown as his bare legs. His dark
hair clustered thickly around his face, which
had a curious vivacity of expression that seemed
to change each moment.

A red woollen sash fastened about his
thighs distinguished him from the other boys.
Only the next day the monk had reason to
remember the bright-colored sash, for, as he
was strolling toward the quiet corner of the
orchard, he saw it half-way up one of the
cherry-trees like a banner waving in the wind.
Its wearer meanwhile was enjoying the ripe,
red fruit, but his feast came abruptly to an end
when he saw the dark robe and white mantle

of the Prior coming toward him. He jumped
nimbly to the ground, then stumbled and fell.
He felt the Prior's hand upon his shoulder—
he was no coward, but this time it was safe to
tremble. He lay still a moment, when his
curiosity got the better of him, and he opened
his dark, bewildered eyes. But the face he
looked into was not unkind, yet he was very
glad it was the companion-monk's cassock that
he pulled yesterday.

"I was so hungry," he wailed.

The monk lifted the boy to his feet and
began to stroke back the soft, dusky curls.
"Next time come to the refectory, instead of
over the walls like a thief," he said, a little
sternly. "You may go, Filippo—I have seen
you before."

The child flushed guiltily. He was as
beautiful as a cherub, and looked quite as
guileless as he gave to the Prior the branch
heavy with cherries.

"No, take them," he said, touched by the
child's honor, and Lippo scampered away.

At times he would be gone from home all
3

night, sleeping on straw in a box, faring as best he could for food—but oftener during the day, for hours, was hungry and cold. Yet what were these discomforts—how easily forgotten—in the joy of freedom and adventure!

But how different life at the Carmine would be. Little Lippo knew that, as he listened to his aunt's story of himself to the monks—of the orphan whose father, her brother, had died when the boy was two years old, and his mother shortly after his birth. She had done the best she could for the child, but now it was no use, she could support him no longer; she must bring him to them to educate; she trusted the good Brothers would find the lad obedient and promising.

The Prior had been watching the boy while Mona Lapaccia was speaking, and recalled the incident of the street and the orchard; Lippi, too, on seeing him, had instantly remembered it, but as ever the quick, light-hearted child appeared to be wholly ignorant of any mischief.

" Has he been allowed often in the street?" the Prior asked, looking straight into Mona

Lapaccia's eyes when she had finished. It was no use for her to conceal the truth, so it was all confessed.

"We shall do what we can with him," he said kindly, and Lippi was left in the Carmine.

But all the monks were not like the Prior. There was a gentleness in his manner when he took Filippo by the hand and led him into his cell that quite won the boy's heart. He had always thought of the monks as selfish, disagreeable men, and the boys of the street laughed at them so. Then, too, the Prior did not mention the incident of the day before.

"There are several boys here already," he said, "and so you will not be alone. This is my cell, and whenever you wish to see me about any thing you will find me here. Come, we will go to your master." He held out his hand to Filippo, and they passed through the bare cell, with its stone walls and one window, furnished only with a small bed and a rough bench, upon which lay an illuminated manuscript, through the dark refectory with its two long tables, to the court-yard.

Six boys, all two or three years older than Lippo, were amusing themselves at the fountain, while one, a little younger than the rest, was sitting on a bench beside a monk who was instructing him in drawing uncials. The Prior led Filippo to a tall, grave-looking monk, who gave him a book to study. Every thing was so new and strange that he could not keep his eyes on his lesson, and he was glad when the refectory bell sounded for the noonday meal. The boys formed in procession, and Lippo's companion was Diamante, a handsome lad with eyes full of dreams and mouth full of smiles —the very one Lippo watched in the morning drawing such fascinating letters on parchment.

So they marched to the dark refectory and took their places at the end of one of the long tables.   How silent, and solemn, and dreary it all was.   Lippo longed to be free, and when night came and he was alone in his cell, he buried his face in the rough covering of his couch and sobbed himself to sleep.

The days went on. Filippo was not a favorite with his master, and the monks found it was useless to try to make a scholar of him.

No amount of penances were sufficient punishment to keep him from spoiling his books by making little figures all over them. One day his master complained to the Prior. He came and took up one of the disfigured manuscripts. Filippo stood with downcast eyes, expecting a severer rebuke than before. The Prior looked down upon him and said nothing, but took him by the hand and led him to another monk, the very one who was teaching Diamante to draw.

Fra Anselmo looked at his new pupil, and saw in him something more than the wild, frolicsome boy that had so disturbed the other friars.

"Come," said Fra Anselmo with a smile, "sit by me and we will see what you can do. Diamante draws very well, can you?" and he held the parchment before Lippo, who had climbed on to the bench.

Very often, when at home, and impatient to be on the street, the boy had beguiled the time with pictures on the door—and yet Mona

Lapaccia had never noticed them more than to say he must not deface the walls.

"Let me see you draw these uncials," said Fra Anselmo as he set a copy for Lippo. The boy took the pen, and with a few rapid strokes made the letters. His skill seemed to surprise the master, and he set him a more difficult copy, but Lippo drew with the same ease. Again the monk seemed astonished, and after a few more tests he broke out, as if in half soliloquy: "I thought Diamante the most skilful boy I had ever seen——" but he did not finish.

As he drew, Fra Anselmo told him stories about pictures in the chapel which he had so often longed to stand before and look at,—so beautiful to him that he had often thought of them as he lay awake in his cell or fell asleep only to dream of them.

The next morning he spent the first hour after mass with Fra Anselmo in the chapel. It had been newly painted by Masaccio, and the Prior said Fra Anselmo would find in these pictures many lessons to teach. There were the

Coronation, and the stories of the saints.
The boys always welcomed the hour, and recently Fra Anselmo had suggested that they
try to draw the various figures in outline. It
was Diamante who, though the youngest, had
won the special interest of the master. But
now a new genius was in the Carmine. Fra
Anselmo had recognized that the moment
Lippo had made the first uncial with that grace
and accuracy which bespoke the true talent.
It was with special interest that the monk
watched the effects of the beautiful paintings
upon the boy. Instantly the child seemed to
catch the peculiar charm of the great artist.
How different were these pictures, unfinished
though they were, from the lifeless, artificial
frescos in Florence. How often Fra Anselmo
had wandered into the churches that he might
find some real living picture that would speak
humanity. The very spirit of Masaccio, which
appealed so strongly to him, had found its way
to the boy's soul. Yet he was only a child,
and Fra Anselmo would not judge too quickly.
He led Lippo into the cloister where he might

see the Consecration. He watched the boy as he drew the rude outlines, and again the child's talent was evident.

"Have you ever painted?" asked Fra Anselmo.

"Only a few weeks when I was under the master in the city; I found a brush and daubed my books so I could not read. He taught me my letters—he did not care about the pictures —he would not let me draw. But it is the color I love so."

Indeed it seemed as if he were born with a subtle and perfect instinct for coloring, and detected a false line as quickly as the master himself.

Already the Prior had heard of the child's talent, for Fra Anselmo was not one to keep so great a discovery to himself. Several mornings after, the Prior entered the chapel, and coming to where Lippo was painting with the materials Fra Anselmo had provided, looked over the boy's shoulder. It was the coloring—the genius that seemed to recognize the peculiar beauty of harmony—that appealed to the Prior.

" What if the poor Carmine convent should have within its walls such a spirit as had made the Dominicans of San Marco famous. To think what Fra Angelico has done for the preaching friars. Who knows but this merry child, who seemed so good-for-nothing the other morning, may not one day do as much for us?" thought the Prior as he watched the little hand working so eagerly at the canvas. "Fra Anselmo is right in encouraging the boy."

And so Filippo was allowed the use of the chapel ; the little Diamante was his constant companion. As the months wore away the old restlessness and longing often came upon him, and he would chafe and grow pale under the seclusion. Then too he would fire Diamante and some of the other boys with a desire for freedom, by his tales of old adventures.

"Ah!" he would cry, "to be in the world again !" But Fra Anselmo watched him carefully, and although he often exclaimed against the confinement, there was a love and interest in his work, which kept him from deserting.

Once or twice he had found his way outside the convent, but he usually came back at night hungry and humbled.

After Filippo had been in the convent a year and colored to his heart's content, he began a real painting in fresco in one corner of the chapel. It was in the cloister near Masaccio's Consecration. He worked at it faithfully, day by day, with a patience that surprised Fra Anselmo, for so often before he had known the boy to throw down his brush and leave the coloring. But this was a real picture,—and when the Prior came into the chapel to watch the progress, and the monks too would steal in, it gave him a sense of gratification in the work which inspired him to greater carefulness.

But this was not the only picture ; others were gradually finished, and when the months had lengthened into years, the monastery was variously adorned with saints and Madonnas painted there by the young Carmelite genius.

"Surely the spirit of Masaccio has entered the soul of Filippo,"—so every one said who saw the work of the young artist.

Could any thing be more life-like than his San Maziale, on the pillar near the organ !

It was Fra Anselmo who guided the impetuous boy, and now that nine years had passed the master was more than realizing his expectations. Many praises poured upon Lippi. He heard already how the Dominicans were fearing the rival of their great painter. The convent bounds were becoming too narrow for him. He longed to be out in the great world. Could he not paint his wonderful pictures there—nay more beautiful !

There was so much in the convent life that was unpromising to art. The espousals of piety and poverty, the inexplicable mysteries, martyrdoms, ascetic faces and haggard figures, morbid enthusiasm and spiritual frenzy, were repugnant, yes, painful to Filippo. Absence of beauty was almost a deformity with him. Sad-visaged penitents, men scourging themselves, prostrate in prayer, wrestling with demons, awoke no responsive chord in his breast, nor stimulated his artistic spirit. The joylessness of early Christian art was incompatible with his gladsome temperament. He did not believe in making art the handmaid of religion that had for its message the doctrine of fear. His pictures should never be of that kind.

"Pain is deformity,—ecstasy is not sanctity," he replied one day to a monk who chided him for drawing a round-limbed smiling saint; "the lack of physical beauty is a misfortune—not every woe-begone monk is a martyr-saint, nor every pensive nun an angel."

The monk drew back, and sanctimoniously made the sign of the cross; was the Prior right, could this strong-headed boy, drawing bright-colored, alluring figures, ever glorify the Church of the Carmine and exalt the Order?

"I wonder," laughed Lippi to Diamante, as the Brother went from the painting in pious horror, "if he will cover his eyes in Paradise when he beholds the glorified bodies of the saints?"

Yet all was not repulsive in the life around Fra Lippi. There were men among the monks whose broad shoulders, singularly brilliant dark faces, and magnificent pose, would inspire a less artistic soul than his. Then, too, there were those men like the Prior and Fra Anselmo, upon whose features had settled that beautiful, soft calm of those who had kept themselves unspotted from the world. Lippo felt its unspeakable charm, apart from him though it was. There was a combination of the beautiful with the awful, the gentle with the implacable.

He knew, too, that the life of the cloister was not all disagreeable and repelling. In the damp dark walls were thoughtful, gentle souls, whose home in the change of fortunes and oppression of wars could be in no other place. Their life was a busy one. There were men of the noblest, gentlest blood, from whom came the example of courtly manners, polished speech, and refined taste. Through the years of the desolation and ruin that war brought they preserved art, literature, and religion,

and infused into civilization the principle of
piety, self-sacrifice, chastity, and charity ; they
declared a message that protested against vio-
lence, injustice, wars, and luxury; they re-
vealed bright glimpses of the promised reward
for the triumphant martyr.

Fra Lippi felt no need of such a refuge, no
need of the sanctity of solitude. It was enough
that the cloister had preserved the blessed art
traditions and legends. But now with so little
freedom terrible superstitions were nurtured.
It narrowed the bounds of art. To the restless soul of Lippi, it seemed that the time had
come when seclusion ceased to be a necessity.

Despite the entreaties of Fra Anselmo, he
took matters in his own hands, and one night
the Prior found Lippi's cell empty. Even
though he left the convent he wore the habit of
a Carmelite monk,—and assured Fra Anselmo
that he would bring as much honor—nay more
—to the Order, as if he remained in the
Carmine.

He was free !

Ah ! the world,—the bright, joyous world

so full of sunshine. And Florence ! what had
he ever known of that hill-encircled city. How
fair were its flowery fields, its pearl villas, its
spires and towers, the sparkling Arno spanned
by its graceful arched bridges. What an enchanted land this was, contrasted with the
shadowy courts of the Carmine, its dusky
shrubbery and funereal cypresses. There he
had seldom seen the golden sunlight, or felt
its warmth. It could hardly force its way to
the convent through the tangled growth of
trees. The very ground was too damp for
grass to grow,—only now and then a flower-
stock or rose-bush struggled for existence.
Even the walls of the convent were a cold
gray ; many of its dark corners were covered
with green mould—and the damp interior—
ah ! the memory of it made him shudder even
in the sunshine.

At first it was pleasure enough to wander
outside the city, to lie on some Tuscan hill-
side half lost in the tangle of vines and blossoms, to watch the sweep of scythes in the
breast-high grasses, to sketch the lithe, brown-

armed and strong-limbed youths and maidens
carrying baskets of grapes in vintage time;
to go singing in the moonlight with merry
companions, to laugh, to jest, to paint beautiful faces, to bask in the sunshine of smiles,
to sip wine in dukes' houses,—this was life
indeed!

And the wonderful glow of color of the
Carnivals was like some fairy-land enchant-
ment to him. The gayly dressed multitude
that thronged the squares and piazzas; the
brilliant processions, the mass of scarlet, blue,
and gold outlined against the dull stones of
palaces and cathedrals; the flowers, the music,
the bon-bons, the jewels, the mystery of masks,
the flashing smiles, the tumult and confusion,
the mirth, the mischief; the wild, the fantastic, the laughter, the freedom,—ah! life!—
it was a merry holiday!

Ah, Florence! .fair and charming! The
noise of war was now hushed. He could
listen to the story of palace and cathedral,—
to him the very stones were eloquent with
legends of the past. Here, along the Borgo

Santi Apostoli, were stone and iron palaces, the strongholds of the Lamberti, and Uberti, and Amidei, and Buondelmonte. From the windows and towers of these noble houses were carried on private wars, before the families separated into factions and styled themselves Guelph and Ghibelline.

Here, through the Ponte Vecchio, one sunny Easter morning, Buondelmonte richly dressed in white, came riding on his white horse. Here, by the statue of Mars, the coward Uberti struck him—and Arrigo, and Lamberti, and Amidei hastened to cut his throat,—for no greater reason than that Buondelmonte had resented an insult to a friend at a banquet not long before. It was a pity his dagger did not find Oddo's heart, at the table that day; then he would never have promised—that the quarrel might end—to marry Oddo's ugly niece and broken his faith and plighted it to Beatrice Donati. Here, through the streets and squares, through the Piazza della Signoria, Buondelmonte's funeral car was drawn, while in it Beatrice sat, holding her lover's head, her bridal robes soaked with blood.   Then the fury, the horror, the tumult, the burning, the butchering, the banishing!

From this house, near that of the Donati, the sad eyes of a poet seemed to look.   In the little church of San Martino, that poet was married to Gemma Donati.   Across the street, "a saintly maiden," Beatrice Portinari, lived and died.

Here, in the Piazza San Pier Maggiore, Corso Donati was summoned by the Podestà to answer for his treasons.   Here were the streets filled with the shower of stones and arrows which were aimed at his besiegers. Ah, the evil times of the Bianchi and Neri!

What tales of wrath, and war, and fury that bell in the Vecchio tower could tell!   How often Lippi had heard the bell of the Carmine summon men to arms, instead of prayers !   But there was another bell tower which whispered of a calm valley, even while Florence was rent by strife—a gentle slope where a shepherd boy used to lie, and draw figures of his feeding sheep.   How much more glorious this tale !

If Diamante were only with him! If he too would leave the Carmine! He would be his teacher—he would take him to this Campanile, together they would stand before the delicate tracery that enriched its windows, they would speak to the four Evangelists standing in simple majesty on the western side. They would go to the Baptistry and stand before those marvellous gates, and read their stories in bronze,—ah! what poetic touches were there! He could lay his hand on them—he could feel the wonderful workmanship! The portals of Paradise could not be more beautiful! They would go to Santa Croce and study the reliefs of its vaulted ceiling.

It was the works in terra cotta and marble that pleased Filippo most. He never tired of the singing, dancing children of Lucca della Robbia. He would always study the workers in plastic arts! But first he must see the other cities of Italy. Then came the year of wandering.

What had he known of the life he renounced

that first year in the Carmine. He would see something of the world—he loved it! It was cruel to extort such vows. He would never go back to the monastery—he hated it! Then the passionate nature yielded to the temptations. How easy for a spirit like his to attract souls given over to the pleasures of life. They would be his friends, and he theirs. The world was bright, and happy, and joyous. He could forget painting for a while. That was good enough for a convent, and he loved it there. Now he was different. His purse was large enough for a little merriment.

But quickly the joy and freedom came to an end on that unfortunate day when he was with his friends in a boat, at Ancona, and the Moorish galley had led them captives to Barbary. Ah! then he longed for the beautiful sunlit hills of Fiesole—yes, perhaps for the convent of the Carmine. Any thing was better than this captivity—despite the purple wine and white grapes the slave brought him, —in spite of the dreamy languor of the Mediterranean. In the midst of soft winds he

longed to see the distant snow-capped peaks
of the Apennines.

Yet that mishap, after all, was the beginning
of his good fortune.   He did not know it then.
What was it that should have suggested to
him the opportunity to draw the full-length
figure on the wall of his master's house ?   How
quickly he had seized the piece of charcoal
that fell from the fire and pictured the chief,
robed in his Moorish vestments.

Then came freedom and friendship, thanks
to his blessed gift of painting.   How the old
love rushed back upon him !   Now his dreams
were coming true.

From Barbary to Naples,—to Florence,—
to fame !

The news of the great Cosmo de Medici's
interest in Fra Lippi reached the convent.
The wayward Brother had brought both disgrace and honor to their Order.   Whenever
he went back to the Carmine for a day, the
monks greeted him as the boy whom they had
scolded and petted.   In their narrow life,
these holy men could not realize the power of

other influences than those of the Carmine upon such a temperament as Lippi's. Little did they know their artist as he came back to them. They felt that he should now remain at the convent which had been his boyhood home, and be the more eager as the great opportunities were opening in the city, to add honor to the Carmelite Order.

Ah ! be again imprisoned, after he had once escaped—again illuminate manuscripts, and teach convent boys to draw uncials? Diamante might be satisfied to stay, but with Lippi painting was a soul-passion, demanding expression. It was no mere stepping-stone to personal favor with princes, or the praise that he might bring to that which he represented. He cared less and less for what men might say, for those who praised or those who scoffed at his realism.

Impulse guided him. Here was true pleasure. As in painting, so in life—he had proved it.

Life had changed to him since those days at the Carmine. To think he had been content to remain as long as he did! Now it was not the scanty fare of the refectory tables, and sacred services, but those things which satisfied the body and soul.

Ah! it was more; it was the old spirit of boyhood back again, when he might wander where he pleased,—the satisfied joy of freedom.

V.

NE morning after mass, the Abbess opened the chapel door and saw Lippi sitting dejectedly before the altar, his brush thrown down, his cowl awry, the face of the Madonna with a streak of dark paint across it. As he glanced up, the Abbess missed the bright look with which he had always greeted her. He said nothing. The Abbess waited for him to speak.

At last he looked up at her. " It is utterly useless—I can see no face whereby I gain inspiration."

The Abbess was shocked. If he would not pray, perhaps he would go and stand before

56

one of Giotto's sad-smiling Madonnas ? But
Lippi only shrugged his shoulders.

" Art deals with the heart, the imagination,
not with visions, nor long-eyed Madonnas
and lifeless saints. A fine way to paint the
soul by painting the body ill ! " A deeper look
of melancholy came into his face than the
Abbess supposed could ever be there. " I
would these fingers could guide this brush as
the heart dictates,—the form and idea must be
harmonious in order to satisfy."

He picked up his brush and sighed ; his
impatience was gone. If he was a hot-headed
Florentine, the Abbess saw there was something very sweet and gentle withal. She left
him painting the folds of the long white robe.

A few days later Fra Lippi stood at the
door of the Abbess' withdrawing-room. He
had come to consult her in regard to further
ornamentation of the moulding above the
chancel, for having postponed the painting of
the Madonna face, he was meanwhile devot-
ing the time to relieving the sombreness of the

walls.   As he stood waiting he heard the murmur of voices, then a hush, then the nuns'
voices rose in this jubilant hymn of springtide :

> Plaudite cœli,
> Rideat æther,
> Summus et imus
> Gaudeat orbis.
> Transcivit atræ
> Turba procellæ ;
> Subiit almaæ.
> Gloria palmæ.
>
> Surgite verni,
> Surgite flores,
> Gemina pictis ;
> Teneris mixtæ
> Violis rosæ
> Candida sparsis
> Lilia calthis.

There was one voice he distinguished from
the others, so rich and melodious that it might
belong to Saint Cecilia herself.   In a moment
the door opened, and from the place where he
stood he could see only one of the nuns, and
she was bending over an altar-cloth embroid-

ery, so her face was half hidden. He quickly
stepped back as the Abbess came forward to
meet him, and in his desire to speak with her
he would not have noticed the young girl a
second time—her robe made her seem so simi-
lar to the many nuns, all of whom were so
much alike, he had often declared to himself,
—but she lifted her head, and her eyes met his
a single moment. This face he had seen before,—yes, in Florence. Yet why she should
now be in Prato, and above all things at the
convent of Santa Margharita, surprised him
greatly.

As Lippi walked with the Abbess to
the chapel, he found himself wondering more
and more what the circumstances were that
brought Lucrezia Buti to the convent. Indeed he was so silent that the Abbess was
obliged to remind him that there was something he had said he wished to consult with
her about.

" Ah," he replied, speaking rapidly as if his
thoughts were elsewhere, " it was about the
moulding,"—and he began describing the gen-

eral plan that had occurred to him for coloring
the walls. He would bring two of his pupils,
Fra Diamante and Sandro Botticelli, — of
course all this was to be subordinate to the
altar decorations, yet the good effect would be
so much heightened by the particular attention given to the surroundings. And in regard
to the moulding, should not that be particularly bright?

As Lippi spoke with the Abbess, he pointed
out to her some of his work, for by this time
they had entered the chapel and were in
sight of the altar. They had both crossed
themselves as they caught a glimpse of the
candle burning perpetually before the crucifix,
and when they reached the chancel railing
the Abbess, turning her glance from the wall
on the left, was surprised to see that Lippi
had painted the Madonna face. As she
stepped forward for a better view, Lippi inter-
cepted her by hastily drawing his brush across
it. Yet she had seen enough to feel that she
would not like the Madonna, but she was disappointed to have it destroyed.

"No! No!" she cried, as if she could stop the artist with her outstretched arms; "let me see it, I pray thee."

It was too late, and the disfigured face was all that remained of the realistic painting of a moment before. The Abbess knew that it had been very life-like,—yet the face looking down at her might belong to any peasant girl.

Lippi stood a long time before speaking.

"You know," he said at last, "my master uses models."

The Abbess said nothing, yet she had given up all hope of Lippi's ever being able to reproduce the ideal.

"There must be some one in the convent," —he hesitated as the vision of the beautiful face bending over her gold embroidery swept before him. The Abbess was thinking of that same face.

Lucrezia Buti had been in the convent but a short time, yet her gentle ways and loveliness had won the heart of the Abbess from the very first. To be sure she had not yet

taken the vows of a nun, but she would in
time, for she had told the Abbess that she had
left Florence that her life might be an ideal
one drawn from that of St. Agnes. She certainly had turned her back upon one of the
richest nobles, to avoid a marriage with him,
—and the Abbess sympathized with that.

"Is there no one?" she heard Lippi again
question, and she started from her reverie.
"Yes," he continued, "is not Lucrezia Buti
here,—she comes from Florence, does she
not?"

The Abbess was never more sorely perplexed. Yet what danger was there? Lippi
was a holy Frate from the Carmine,—true he
left the convent years ago—but he was young
then—in fact she did not understand it very
well—she must ask Father Antonio. Lippi
wore the robe of a monk and painted sacred
pictures. To be sure, she had been deeply pre-
judiced against him, but she felt that she
wronged him. Natures were so different—he
seemed too full of life to find a cloister com-
fortable,—and the Abbess knew that they

were not always the holiest men who stayed in monasteries.

She thought of all the nuns, but ever the rapt expression of Lucrezia came before her.

" Yes," she said, drawing a long breath— " she is here " ; she paused.

" May I not perform mass to-morrow ?" he asked.

Indeed why should he not ? Had he not been chaplain for a convent of nuns,—and rector of St. Quirico only the year before ? If Father Antonio should happen to come from Florence, why, all the better. They could talk over the matter that had from the beginning made her so much trouble.

In the morning the nuns looked at the new Frate, and some way they all seemed to know that it was Lippo Lippi—what other monk had so bright a smile or so buoyant a step ! Yet why they should recognize him no one could say, for even as the Abbess had decreed, their only glimpse of the outer world had been from the windows of their rooms, since the staging had been put up in the chapel.

Through the chanting of the Kyrie, the Credo, the Sanctus, and the Agnus Dei, he heard the same deep rich voice that had so thrilled him the day before.

When the host was raised and all the nuns were on their knees, one face alone was uplifted, and Lucrezia looked into the dark, limpid eyes of Lippo Lippi.

Lucrezia Buti, whom Fra Lippi was so greatly surprised to see among the nuns, was from a noble Florentine family. He had seen her the year before at the Grand Duke's palace. He saw her once after that standing near the Campanile. He had heard that she was to be betrothed to Senor Aletri of the princely house of Strozzi. He had always thought her the most beautiful of all the beautiful women he had ever seen,—and with them Italy blossomed like a garden. He remembered the night he first saw her,—how the saintly purity of her face distinguished her from the glittering women around her. He remembered in what graceful folds her white robes fell from the

square-cut neck to her feet; how the over-
sleeves hung open from the shoulder and
showed the dainty lace sleeves wrought with
gold thread,—through the thin stuff he could
see the pink flesh tints of her arms. Her face
seemed to him more Venetian than Florentine,
with its delicately rounded chin, its full flexible
lips, the rippling, red-gold hair, and the deep
brown eyes over which long lashes curled.

He remembered how that night he had
refused to go singing carnival songs with the
youths of the city; how they, heated with wine,
had jeered and taunted him by asking if he
were turning pious monk. How he went to
the Carmine that night instead of his own
apartments; how the face of the old Friar
lighted when he opened the door and saw who
it was at that late hour, wishing admittance.
How the Friar talked and talked about the
sins of the world, and the lust of the flesh, and
prayer, and penance. How, as he sat there,
the Friar thought he was listening, instead of
thinking of a smile of divine sweetness, and a
face fairer than that of the Holy Virgin look-
5

ing out at him from the canvas, beautiful in colors, put there by the hand of Masaccio. How the Friar would have crossed himself and implored protection from the temptations of the devil, if he had known that Lippi's thoughts were of a woman.

Then he went to his old cell, that night, and when he lay down on the bare, hard boards that served for a bed and a pillow, a revulsion of thoughts came over him. To be in the very cell where years before the Prior had led him for the first words, was like living over again the old days, and Lippi felt how he had outgrown them. The very air was stifling.

The convent was never his choice. It was almost forced upon him. He remembered how he hated his books and studies, and used to draw little figures all over the leaves. He shuddered as he thought of the long fasts, the night prayers, and penance. He detested his work, he abominated his confinement, he loathed his vows.

He could hear the wind sighing just as it used to so many years ago, and a gust from the cracks around the window made the taper flare and throw gigantic shadows. He put out the light and closed his eyes. He was no longer in his narrow cell, but lying in a ship bound with cords, looking up into the night sky, and the stars were shining down in his eyes. A Moor came and rudely kicked him ; then a low-browed woman seemed to step from the canvas he was painting and offer him a glass of wine; it was a beautiful deep red, like the velvet gown she wore, but as she came nearer he could see dregs in the bottom of the glass. Yet he took it smilingly from her hand and put it to her lips ; the flush left her cheek and a great horror came to her eyes, which changed to triumph as she looked beyond him; he turned to see a tall, slender maiden with red-gold hair; she stretched her arms towards him, and there were tears in her sorrowful eyes, but he dreamed no more,—he remembered that the matin bell awoke him.

Since then he had been in the bowers of gay ladies, whose black hair, lustrous eyes, and luring smiles came back to him now. He had given the dark face of that low-browed woman to Herodias, in the Prato Cathedral.

Ah! but that other face with the light of truth in its smile! He would paint that face; yes, by the saints and martyrs, he would be near those blessed eyes, and hear that low voice speak to him!

VI.

Y daughter," said the Abbess to Lucrezia, a few mornings later, "I would see you ; come with me."

The color faded in Lucrezia's cheeks. Could it be that her father had sent for her—or possibly the Abbess was going to urge her taking the vows ?

" My daughter, even though you were born in the heat and flare of a worldly city, its dust has never profaned you ; it is as though you were a modest flower growing in hidden places." Lucrezia paled still more ; she shrank from the very thing she sought when entering the convent.

" There are women whom the Lord has crowned with beauty," continued the Abbess, " a divine loveliness like that of Mary, his mother, and they know it not."

Lucrezia's eyes drooped, a wave of color came back to her cheeks.

" My daughter, your beauty was not given to adorn a Florentine palace, and then grow sorrowful and faded by the burdens of that dissolute city; it was not given you for your own enjoyment, or to win a lover—— " (Oh! Abbess Margharita, your voice is a little tremulous, and a dewy look comes into your violet eyes as you remember how, under the almond trees, Francesco, your lover, took you in his arms, whispering such sweet words about your beautiful face, kissing your hair, your eyes, your cheeks, your mouth, your throat, around which he fastened a string of pearls.)

" No," she said as the vision passed, and the weary years of convent life, made sacred by her prayers and tears, came to her, " your beauty is like a fair flower to be laid at the

shrine of the Holy Virgin." (Oh! Lucrezia
Buti, you tremble as you strive against the
thought that the convent of Santa Margharita
has become less sweet a shelter during the last
few days!) "My daughter," she heard the
Abbess say, "you know that these are trou-
blous times, and the pious ones look into the
future and cover their eyes. The Virgin and
saints are no longer painted by prayerful
monks. Art, that was to be the handmaid
of religion, has been so far debased that pictures of shameless women, in the guise of our
Blessed Lady, are not only hung in palaces by
profligate princes, but are bought for cathedrals. Think of the Mother of all Purity
being thus presented for the worshipping
people."

Lucrezia silently looked at the Abbess.

"It has been decided that in you, the Frate
who is painting the altar-piece of the Madonna
Cintola, and who has so lately come from Florence, where he sees not the image of our Lady
in the jewelled women, who think of nothing
but amours and laughter,—in you he finds

such beauty that he shall paint your face for the Madonna."

"Oh, no! no!" cried Lucrezia, her heart beating so wildly that it seemed as if the Abbess must see how it sent the blood burning in her cheeks, and guess her reason for hesitating.

"My daughter, would it not be blessed indeed if through your sweetness and grace the penitent and faithful be reminded of Mary? Father Antonio and I have so decided this morning. Go, child, to your room, and pray before the image of the Virgin that she may fill your heart with her spirit and angelic loveliness."

Lucrezia went to her room and sat by the open window. Was it for this she had sought repose in the convent of Santa Margharita? She had never forgotten the aquiline outline of that artist's face,—the dark eyes with their dreaming lids, the smile as frank as sunlight. But he was a monk,—and she had come to a convent. Could it be that the laughter and hints and coarse jokes of the Florentines were true—had he disgraced his vows? It could not be that he was so profligate, for the Abbess would never allow the face of the Virgin to be painted by an unworthy hand. Fra Angelico had been chosen to do the work, and she was sure no dishonored successor would be tolerated in the sacred chapel of Santa Margharita.

Lucrezia laid her head on the low, broad window-frame, and looked into the garden. The cherries glowed in bright spots against the dark-green leaves, and the grapes hung with · their purple sides ripening in the sun. The water flashed in the fountain. Below in the meadow Florence lay; she could almost see the stone walls of her father's palace.

How different were the bare walls and hard furniture of the convent from the frescoed ceilings, the gilded chairs, the marble floors, and brilliant tapestry cloths, of her home. There were rare vases, and statues, and pictures; she glanced at the little bed and thought of her own couch hung with peacock satin embroidered with gold. She thought of her gown

of soft silk, and pearl girdle, for which she
had taken the coarse robe of a novice, the rosary and cross.   But she could not lay aside
the torments of the world with her garment—
they followed her to sacred places.   She prostrated herself before the image of the Virgin ;
ought she to seek her confessor,—she could
not lay bare her heart with this secret, to even
him.   "O blessed Mother," she prayed, "let
me love but thee."

VII.

HE next morning the Abbess went to Lucrezia's room.

"The Frate is waiting for us," she said, "and it is arranged that you shall sit for him two hours each morning. He has asked for part of the afternoon too, but that is not fully settled. I shall, of course, accompany you and remain with you. He has asked that you wear a white robe,—some garment that falls from the throat in graceful folds."

For a moment Lucrezia hesitated as if in doubt whether the Abbess would allow the change, but seeing that she had considered the matter already and implied her consent, she hastened to lay aside her nun's habit for the one gown she had brought with her,—a

75

memorial of the gayety at Florence, of the days
before the renunciation,—a simple dress in its
time and place, neither brilliant nor ostenta-
tious.   It was   one   of those   delicate silks
which give to the wearer a peculiar grace and
sweetness.   Its fashion seemed to belong particularly to Lucrezia, whose refined and in-
stinctive breeding had always been so charming
to men.   She had brought this garment with
her to the convent, knowing, of course, she
should have no use for it, but reluctant to part
with what seemed so much a part of herself.
When the Abbess first saw it, carefully laid
away with the little store of personal posses-
sions which Lucrezia had unpacked, she was
slightly disturbed, but then, seeming to recall
how much the fair one from Florence had sac-
rificed for the dreariness of Santa Margharita's
said no more than gently to remind the novice
of all that was required in a life of renunciation.

It was   a fair picture that greeted Lippi
when glancing from his work in the chancel, he saw the chapel door open and two
figures enter : the Abbess, tall, dark, and

sombre in the garb of her order; Lucrezia,
so beautiful, so flower-like in contrast. And
the gown—the artist's eye had seen that,—the
white robe falling from the square-cut neck to
the feet; the thin, transparent lace heightening
the soft flesh flush of her throat, and modestly
veiling the sweet beauty of the bosom so vir-
ginal in form; the over-sleeves, open from the
shoulders, showing the daintily gold-embroidered sleeves, and, through the thin stuff, the
pink tints of her arms. How well he remembered that gown—the very one she had worn
that night in Florence, at the Grand Duke's
palace.

Already the Abbess and Lucrezia were near
him and standing at the railing, but the brief
interval during their walk down the nave had
been so full of recollections that he hardly
dare think of himself in the chapel only to
paint a Madonna, and the beautiful girl as
simply a model. He hastily arranged the canvas upon the easel and stepped forward to
greet the Abbess with that grace and deference
she so much admired.

"I have brought the model, Fra Lippi," she said. "Lucrezia," she continued, turning to the beautiful figure beside her and seeming for the first time to realize the full charm of the girl's face and form, so enhanced by the grace of the gown,—"Lucrezia, this is the painter, Fra Lippi, who requests that you take that position of all others most difficult—the model for the Madonna."

Lucrezia looked at him with a straight-forward yet modest gaze, that contradicted the quick beating of her heart; not that she expected a glance of recognition, for she had not dared hope that Fra Lippi would remember seeing her, even though the memory of the moment when his eyes met hers, that night, thrilled her now. She remembered that he was by the side of her cousin, the Princess Beatrice; her soft clear gaze rested long upon him; there was no other face like his—every feature bore the reflex of an intense, passionate, artistic nature. It was the face she had seen in her dreams, yet she only smiled gently, as she might to any stranger whom she had never met before. Fra Lippi felt a quick disappointed pang, but in his cold and deferential greeting Lucrezia little imagined it a conscious formality which concealed remembrances of an hour which both had lived over since yesterday morning. There was a gallantry and gentleness which Lucrezia did notice withal, and it was not with the courtesy of an ordinary acknowledgment of an introduction that the words were tinged.

" Yonder," said Lippi, "is the place I have planned for you to sit. It is there that I can have the best light. From that window above, the sun seems to come most directly. It is fortunate the chapel was so conveniently arranged."

All this was said with a smile and glance towards the window and eastern side of the chancel, and in a tone quiet and deliberate, which bespoke the man unembarrassed by the thoughts which were crowding his memory.

" Two hours each morning," he continued, "will suffice for the painting, and I trust the work will not be too tiresome for you."

As he spoke he looked at Lucrezia as if he would make her feel the delicacy of the request to the Abbess, that the novice shall devote so much time and weariness to the uninteresting task of becoming a model. During these few moments in which Lippi had indicated the arrangement, previous to the sitting, he seemed to be ever aware of the Abbess' presence and the regard for her opinion. In fact, he spoke almost as if directly to her, and whenever to Lucrezia, included the Abbess' possible modifications of what might be better arranged. The Abbess felt this respect, and found herself more favorably inclined towards the painter than ever before. Lucrezia had already seated herself in the chair to which Lippi had pointed, while he had taken his place before the easel,—the Abbess remaining at the chancel railing.

" Ah, but first if you will stand while I draw the figure full-length—I have painted out my first unhappy effort,—then you can sit while I work on the face of the Virgin. By so dividing the posing I trust that I can make it less wearisome for you," he said, half smiling.

Lucrezia stood erect, with clasped hands. Fra Lippi made a few rapid strokes, then turned to look more directly at her face. What a revelation of beauty, what an inspiration for an artist, what a Madonna he would give to the world! There was a hint of half melancholy in the loving mouth and far-seeing eyes; where the sunshine fell upon her hair it was like burnished gold,—in what rippling shining waves it would float upon her shoulders; there were no shoulders like hers in Florence. What an exquisite figure, what marvellous grace and beauty, what ethereal delicacy!

There was much preliminary sketching to be done. He asked Lucrezia to look up, then down, turn her face to the wall, and then, that he might see the profile from the other side, to look towards the chapel entrance. As she turned towards him for the full-face view, there was a brighter glow in her cheeks, an uplifting of the half-arched brows, and a gentle pressure of the mouth that seemed to please Lippi. He asked her to remain in that position longer than in the others, and

after looking at her intently, as if fascinated by
the picture before him, said, turning towards
the Abbess :

" I think that the best attitude."

" It is very Virgin-like," she replied,—and it
was evident the Abbess felt that this . Madonna would be very real.

After standing awhile at the chancel railing, the Abbess seated herself on one of the
benches near the front, in the left transept.
She drew from her pocket a small piece of silk
and began a bit of embroidery, soon becoming
busily engaged in the handiwork.   Lippi continued at the painting, there was such a delight
in transferring so much beauty to canvas.
The first hour passed quickly.

Lucrezia had been standing so long that Fra
Lippi asked her to rest a few moments.   With
a sigh he leaned back in his chair.   The
Abbess rose from her seat and came to look at
the canvas ; she noticed the glad light in
Lippi's eyes, the suppressed excitement with
which he had painted.   The Abbess was
holding the piece of tapestry in her hand

on which the outlines of The Flight into Egypt were beginning to show. The Abbess was questioning Lippi.

"No, I do not paint Holy Families with Joseph," he smiled; "he is too old and bald;—a pity some of the younger suitor's rods did not blossom."

The Abbess had never heard any one speak this way on sacred subjects, and after the first shock she was rather amused and was tempted to question him more, yet she was fearful of encouraging his irreverence.

"There are beautiful tapestries in Southern Italy, with Greek heads and figures," he was saying; "beauty is the true art principle—the joyous beauty of the Greeks——"

"But the craving for mere beauty is a dangerous thing, my brother." She turned towards the easel : "Our Lady should not be represented in the classic features of a pagan goddess; she should be something more than an idol, a lovely creation that awakens no throb of piety in the breast ; neither should she be stern and motionless, but the most tender, most pure, most sacred Madre, who will be very near the heart of those who salute her as blessed."

Fra Lippi took up his brush again and began to paint. Lucrezia stood in the same position to which he had called the Abbess' attention particularly. The uplifted eyes gave no opportunity for the knowledge of long glances from behind the easel. The Abbess still stood watching Fra Lippi as he painted.

"We have only a hint of the perfection which art will one day reach," Lippi said. "The artist sees the three types—the severe, awful quietude of the Byzantine masters, the pensive sentimentality of Siena, the stately elegance of Florence ; but there must come one who will unite these, and harmonize the human and divine into one great whole." The Abbess stood listening.

"There will be no other one, who, like the saintly Frate, with dreaming eyes will see heaven afar off. The spirit of the times has changed ; the material influence is in advance of the spiritual : the impulse is now for freer drawing, a truer feeling for life-like attitudes and proportion ; the people no longer stand before the bodiless cold Madonnas of Cimabue. We no longer want flat gold backgrounds, but real landscapes, real blue heavens with golden stars. A Virgin with a body should be as worshipful as one without. We paint Mary as a woman. Now, the triumph of the spirit over the body is no longer the all-absorbing theme,—except in monasteries. We can understand why Angelico never used models," —he smiled a little ; " visions came to him like dreams ; his work was the outpouring of his own celestial spirit ; nothing ever disturbed his peaceful meditations. Day after day he was within the white-walled convent, surrounded by cowls and frocks ; day after day he painted the same white-robed souls, whom the burden of flesh no longer oppressed. What did he know of a woman's smile ?"—but Fra Lippi suddenly stopped. The Abbess moved a little uneasily and began to embroider the work which had been idly lying in her lap. Lucrezia looked at Fra Lippi ; his face flushed darkly, his beauti-

ful eyes were dim, his laugh had a sigh in it.
The Abbess said :

"Fra Angelico was, indeed, tenderly shel-
tered from the rude storms of the world. His
paintings are the utterance of a heartfelt love
of spiritual things."

Thus the two hours passed away. The
mellow tone of the bell striking outside the
chapel indicated that the noonday had arrived. The Abbess rose and came forward.
Lippi laid down his brush with a sigh.

"*Eh!* the time has flown quickly!" he said.
"I had no idea my work was so nearly at an
end, this morning. I have not accomplished
as much as I wished—if this afternoon I still
might paint from the model,"—he pushed the
easel towards a better light, and stood looking
at the canvas. "It is such slow work," he
exclaimed, "that soon I shall hope for more
than two hours a day."

As he spoke, he turned from the Abbess to
Lucrezia, who had remained seated. "Do you
find your task a heavy one? It is no easy
thing to be a model—and yet it must give one

Angel
Fra Angelico

pleasure to be thought ideal." He said this as if hardly conscious of the words, in the deeper meaning of his smile.

The blood rioted through Lucrezia's veins. "A heavy task" to stand before him! A wearisome thing to be near him! Ah!—but she could only answer:

"It is you who must be ready to rest; no, I am not weary! I have nothing to do,—it is quite different with you."

"It must be a pleasure to feel that your picture is really begun," said the Abbess.

"Yes," replied Fra Lippi, "the interest will become deeper each day. To-morrow, at the same time, I shall look for you again?" and he spoke directly to the Abbess. "I suppose I must be content with mornings only?"

She hesitated a moment, then hastily said: "Perhaps to-morrow I may be able to decide."

Fra Lippi watched the two women as they passed down the nave. The noonday sun shone through the window above his head, filling the whole chancel with light. How dreary

the chapel was.　It seemed to him as if the
two figures almost disappeared in the darkness.　When the heavy door opened for a
moment he saw them outlined against the sunshine of the court.　He noticed the darkness
all the more after they had gone.

"And so my heart's desire is given me!" he
exclaimed as he threw himself into the chair
where Lucrezia had sat.　"The Virgin is to
be painted with a novice as model.　How I
did dread the noon hour!　But to-morrow I
shall see her again!—My Madonna!"

He wandered out into the court-yard, where
the brightness seemed almost to dazzle him,
after the darkness of the chapel.　He felt restless,—he was unable to paint.

In the afternoon the desire to do nothing
possessed him,—that same feeling which he
had known before in Florence.　It always
came when he thought of her.　He tried for
an hour to finish the predella of the lowest
step.　He threw down his brush in despair.
"It is no use!" he cried.　"The morning is
too long in coming again!　These hours must

be hastened in some other way!" He went out into the court-yard again, where the sunshine of the beautiful afternoon enticed him into the orchard, among the orange-trees and grape-vines.

But whether he was looking into the clear depths of the court-yard fountain, breathing the sweet odor of the violets, or out here with the fruit and leaves, all speaking a thousand things to him, it was the same—the one voice uttering the one thing to his heart.

VIII.

N his restlessness, Lippi thought of Fra Diamante at the Cathedral. He had not visited him as often as he promised since leaving him to paint in the choir. Shortly after they began work together there, Lippi received the commission for Santa Margharita's, and meanwhile Diamante was engaged upon the preliminary outlining and coloring for the frescos.

In Florence, since those days at the Carmine, they had been much together. After Lippi's departure from the convent, Diamante could not remain there contented. He too must break the shackles of that monastic life,

he too must go into the world. Besides he
missed Lippi, whom he followed as his master ;
he wished to be with him—to paint with him.
Soon came the message from his friend, and he
joined him. Months succeeded months more
quickly than they knew, in the pleasure of
painting in palace and church. Yet this without night's gayety would not have been truly
life. Again and again, they were merry companions in Florentine festivities, and more
than once the coarse brown habits with white
cloak and scapular were laid aside for the
cavalier's attire. But now they were in Prato
and separated for the present.

When Lippi entered the Piazza that afternoon, in his walk from Santa Margharita's, he
paused before the Cathedral to again look at
the effect of the curious inlaying of the black
and green serpentine, from Monte Ferrato, al-
ternating with white marble. He was also
attracted to the corner of the façade, where
the pulpit by Donatello projected, whence the
Sacra Cintola preserved in the church was
periodically exposed to the veneration of the

multitude.   Perhaps he observed the beautiful
work the more carefully now that he was espe-
cially interested in the Madonna legends.   At
any rate he never tired of the happy dancing
children, supporting festoons—the seven apartments of exquisite sculptured bas-reliefs.   He
turned towards the entrance to look a moment
at the calm loveliness of Robbia's Madonna;
the plastic arts had the same attraction for him
as when he used to go to Santa Croce and
San Lorenzo, to look at the work of these
masters.

At the sound of voices Lippi turned to see
a group of men come from the side door and
cross the Piazza towards the Via dei Sarti.
He entered the open door and saw Diamante
upon the staging, painting between the pointed
windows of the choir.   As ever, the picturesque interior appealed to the artistic nature ;
the Roman basilica enlarged to the cruciform
shape, with the columns of serpentine and
arches of the nave which belonged to the
original structure ; the Capella della Sacra
Cintola, separated by Brunelleschi's brass

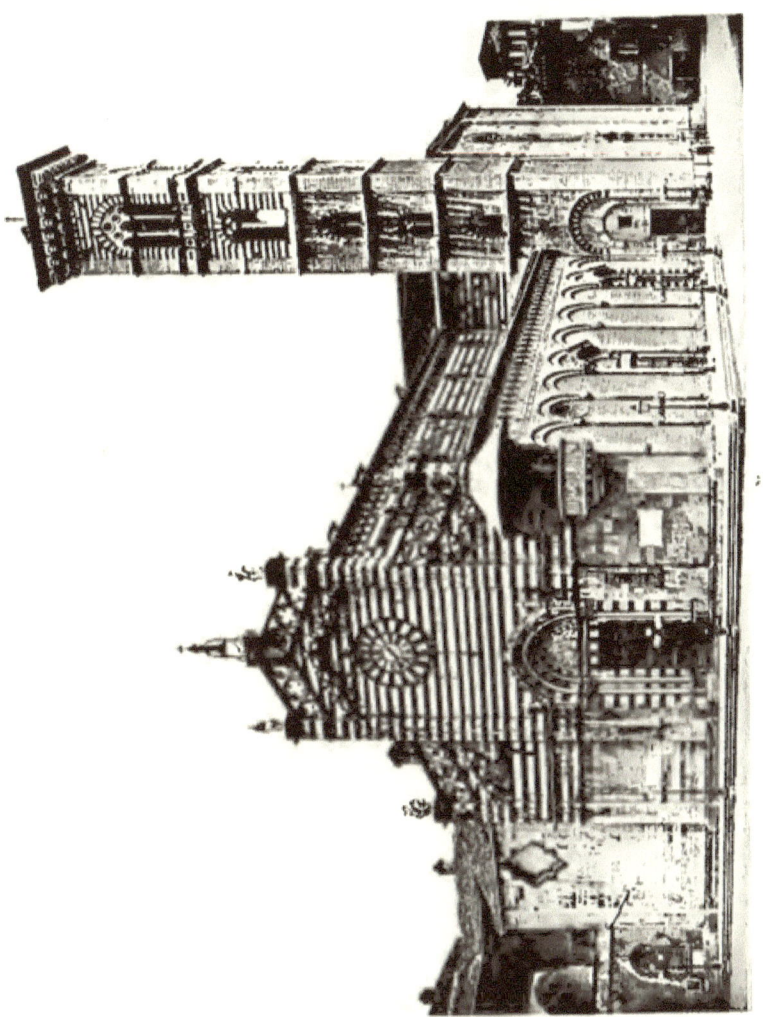

Santo Stefano. (Prato.)

screen ; the circular pulpit with base of carved sphinxes and serpents; in the chancel, the statue of Mary and huge bronze crucifix, so venerated by the Prato worshippers.

"Ah, Diamante !" called a voice below, and the startled painter looked down on the up-turned face of Lippi, who stood beside the high altar. "You would not know who was near though he stayed here till nightfall !" And Lippi laughed heartily, as Diamante with an exclamation of surprise, hastened, palette in hand, to descend the staging.

"Good friar ! So knit to his work !" he continued playfully with his hand upon Diamante's shoulder, after they had exchanged the affectionate greeting. "I have been watching those touches—palette to wall—palette to wall—and never a glance at me."

Botticelli, Diamante's companion, was painting a saint above the *Beheading of St. John.* "Ah, Sandro !" cried Lippi, "that 's not a saint, that 's a nymph—saints have not pout-ing lips breaking into alluring smiles—what round-limbed goddess of Greece have you been dreaming over ? Ah ! my boy, when you paint saints don't let that impetuous imagination run away with you."

Lippi and Diamante stood in the chancel, jesting each other and looking up at the unfinished outlines of the frescos, planning the other wall-spaces of the choir.

" But no more to-day ! " exclaimed Lippi. "Come into the sunshine. There we may talk. Let us together climb Monte Ferrato."

" Only two White Friars," the people said whom they met on the way to Bizenzio Gate, thinking of the austerity of the Carmelite Order, not knowing to what extent the life of these monks was given up to the easy, lighthearted, *debonair* enjoyment of the present. Indeed, Diamante never knew Lippi in a gayer mood. It was a merry time as their talk turned to Florence, and the contrast of the life at Prato. They were already outside the ancient walls of the town, on the road that leads to the foot of the principal peak of Monte Ferrato.

" A few weeks more," said Diamante, laughing, "and there will be two long-faced friars praying till dawn."

Their talk became more serious as they spoke of the frescos at Santo Stefano. "Hardly a day but I see some face in the Piazza I would paint," cried Diamante. "Ah! it is the real flesh and blood that alone brings true inspiration! Yet how hard to work when only what memory recalls is the model. Yesterday I passed a man near the Palazzo del Pretorio. Though I tried so often till eve, it was no use. That face I could not paint. It was the same in Florence."

"It is so," replied Lippi. "The model before one alone can satisfy."

"The Madonna at Santa Margharita's? is it this face—now that face? Yes! I know! The brush will daub!"

They both laughed, and Diamante began recalling what had happened to them so often in Florence. The road turned suddenly to the left, and a mile from Bizenzio Gate had brought them to the foot of Monte Ferrato. They stopped for a little while to note the

peculiar effect of the sandstone, transformed
into red jasper, in contact with the serpentine
limestone.   Passing along the base of the hill,
they found the path leading to the quarries
above, and, after a brisk climb, came upon the
rocks with which they were so familiar, the
blocks of Verdi di Prato, so much used as black
marble in the Florentine churches.

Here, in the clear air of the beautiful afternoon, the town lay stretched out before them,
with the surrounding country and hills. They
found a place farther up in the shade of a tree,
where, upon the moss, they might give themselves up to the pleasing prospect.

"Ah! this is the first time that we have
seen Prato!" said Lippi, as he threw himself
down at full length and leaned upon his arm.
Diamante was seated with his back against
the tree.   "It is well worth our climb."

The afternoon sun threw a mellow light
over all, and flashed in the rippling waters of
the winding Bizenzio.   The old walls with the
Castello dell' Imperatore added to the picturesque scene of the rich, green valley, stretch-

ing far away to the northwest in the direction
of Figline, while Santa Stefano and its Campanile, with the buildings surrounding the
Piazza, rose conspicuously among the dwellings of the town.

" And yonder must be Santa Margharita's ? "
said Diamante, looking in the direction of the
convent, as it stood apart on its little hill.

Lippi had been inquiring the names of some
of the buildings in the vicinity of the Cathedral, and now they had turned toward the
east. The chapel and part of the court were
visible—the rest of the convent half hidden
by the orchard.

" How fare the gay Sisters of the veil, and
their Mother ? Is the Abbess a good keeper
of the pious Carmelite—our second gentle
Angelico ? " and Diamante laughed heartily
as he leaned forward to playfully press the
arm that supported the handsome head.

If Lippi seemed to be serious, it was not
because his thoughts now turned into a new
channel. All the afternoon the same gentle
reverie was present. He lost, for the mo-

7

ment, the sense of being alone, and he was not in the mood to jest. Diamante noticed the change, and was a little perplexed. It was always so different when they used to speak of the convent of St. Ambroggio. " The angels and saints in the altar-piece there would have been innumerable, if Cosimo d'Medici had not come to the rescue," he would say and laugh with Lippi.

"But why not have sent for me before the Palazzo Commission ! I could have painted the fair one !"

" No ! no !"—and so they would jest.

" I know but little of Santa Margharita's," said Lippi, half-smiling, as Diamante began in the old manner ; then, changing quickly the subject, " The Madonna ! It is the most difficult I have yet tried." He did not tell of his restlessness since the noon-day bell, of the sweet thought that the declining sun suggested for the morrow, of something stealing into his heart which he knew so well. There was a calm he loved, here upon the hill, looking down upon the beautiful valley.

"Diamante!" he said, as if the thought
had suddenly occurred to him. "You remember Lucrezia, the daughter of Senor
Buti?"

"The daughter of Francesco Buti?" replied Diamante, unconscious of a tenderness
in Lippi's tone, and unable to see the face
turned from him. "The *Angel* at the Grand
Duke's palace one night, whose praises were
sung me? Forget the fair vision, as told
me? No! no! Ah—ah, I had almost believed there was one lovesick friar in Florence
that night!" He laughed again, and as
Lippi remained silent, continued: "Yet yours
are no blinded eyes, my friend. Yes, she was
beautiful! Did I not see her? What now
of the fair one? Dreaming of Lucrezia in
this dull land?"

Filippo was not in the mood to tell. Was
it strange? Yet often in these hearts where
the one deep, sweet passion is first born,
there is the desire to be alone with the hidden
truth.

"Yes, dreaming!"

"The Princess Beatrice is her cousin," said Diamante. Lippi laughed carelessly, then a shadow came over his face.

"I had not thought," he said.

"Lucrezia is betrothed to Senor Aletri," Diamante was saying. "How unlike the cousins are,—one so fair, the other so dark! The Princess would terrify me; I never understood—yes, understood—but never felt her fascinations."

Filippo made no reply. The conversation flowed easily into other channels.

Had not Francesco Buti recently left Florence? What might be the reason? Had not several nobles gone? And so the monks fell to talking of Florentine affairs in general.

The sun had reached the horizon, and already it was time to return before the darkness steal upon them unawares.

At the Bizenzio Gate, Lippi put his hand gently on Diamante's arm and detained him a moment before they separated.

"It has been an afternoon most pleasant for me," he said, with a smile which the

gathering darkness almost hid. " Our to-
morrow's work will be better for this ram-
ble. Soon I shall return to Santo Stefano.
Meanwhile continue upon the left wall-space.
There is enough planned for the present.
And, Diamante," he added affectionately, as
if loath to part, "again shall we climb Monte
Ferrato? The pious monk!"—and he laughed
gently—" seemed he a little strange to-day?
think you he pines? No! no!" He clasped
Diamante's hand, " Farewell, farewell!" and
as he drew the white mantle closer about him
and disappeared in the gloom, he stopped a
moment and called : " On the hillside again—
perchance I shall have something to tell !"

"What may that be?" thought Diamante,
as he turned into the street that led to his
scantily furnished apartments in a dwelling
not far from the Cathedral. "Whatever it
be, he will tell me! An open heart! A true
friend! How few in this world! A pious
monk! Ah! ah! happy the hours with him !"

But the days passed, and Lippi did not
come. Diamante became impatient.

One morning the Abbess, tired of working
longer on the embroidery, walked up and
down the chapel, then stopped before the side
window and looked out upon the street. She
saw a Carmelite monk coming in the direction
of the convent. She watched him as he came
nearer, and saw him enter the court-yard door.
She turned from the window and slowly
walked towards the chapel door, when it was
opened by the old servant who was followed
by the tall dark monk.

The model ! In a moment it was all solved !
With such loveliness before him, no wonder
the painting was unfinished. Diamante could
scarcely utter the message which had been in
his mind.

"Ah, Diamante!" said Lippi, rising to
greet him, but showing plainly in his face that
he was deeply absorbed in his work.

"I came to tell you," said Diamante, "that
my work at Santo Stefano is finished "—he
spoke hesitatingly,—" and that nothing can
be done until you come." He had approached
the easel and glancing at the model started in
surprise.

"I am yet at work here. I am very busy," replied Lippi, half-smiling, and for a moment looking down at the palette in his hand, with a quick motion of the brush among the colors. "Pardon me, Diamante, I shall come to the Cathedral—I am busy!"

Diamante understood. "Meanwhile I can find something to do," he said, and bowing respectfully to the Abbess, hastened away.

Lucrezia Buti! It was she! How came she there? Never more beautiful than now, thought Diamante. It was this that Lippi would tell him.

He walked back to the Cathedral, but he could not paint. He held his brush idly in his hand and sat looking abstractedly at the frescos. A group of passers-by came in, but the idle, silent painter did not interest them. The long shadows crept in through the windows. The afternoon had fled. Diamante gathered up his colors and left the Cathedral. He went to his apartment,—to the delicate-illuminated texts he used to trace with such fondness. He had often thought there could be no greater pleasure than that of trans-

cribing—to feel the value of precious manuscripts growing day by day as the letters
were finished with exquisite care.   How often
with Fra Anselmo he had worked until dawn,
after night mass, that they might complete
the pages they had begun.   In the Carmine,
one of his duties was to color the uncials, and
he loved the task ; he was proud of his parch-
ments, illuminated as no other in the monastery ; he had now begun a breviary that
would require months of copying, yet when
the midnight bell struck, he sat looking at
the blank page, which, only an evening before,
would have been so fanciful in designs and so
beautiful in colors.

Wherever he looked, whether at the parchment, or the inks, or the pen already between
his fingers, he saw a sheen of gold-red hair,
cheeks the hue of a rose-leaf, and eyes as
tender as the Holy Virgin's.   It affected the
heart like enchanting music.   The hushed
dreams of youth were awakened, and his pulse
bounded at the alarm.

IX.

RA LIPPI painted each day until the light from the eastern window grew too dim to distinguish colors, then with a sigh would lay down his brush. The charm of Lucrezia's face was ever varying—it changed with each passing emotion. Now she was the gentle novice, now the awakened girl in whose eyes was the love-dream, now she was the placid Madonna, now a passion would burn in her cheeks, now the lips curved sadly. Filippo did not know which feature was loveliest. He would look into her eyes and worship their dreamy lustre ; he would look long at the golden light in her hair ; there was her mouth so quivering and sensitive that it seemed formed to kiss rather than to be kissed, but the dimpled corners in which a little shadow hid, the soft curving under the chin,—ah ! that would tempt a stronger monk than Lippi;—Jerome, Anthony,—what a vision was saved them !

Now with that look of divine contemplation she was not less pure than Mary when the wingéd spirit from Paradise came to bring the wondrous message.   Sometime he would paint another Annunziata.   Mary—with Lucrezia's face of course—should kneel with bowed head and downcast eyes before Gabriel, who should bear neither lily nor sceptre, but with folded hands should bow before the Chosen One.   It is the moment she says: " Behold the hand-maid of the Lord." The Ave Maria would always bring this vision to him.

It had been a full month since Lippi began to paint the face of the Madonna ; all else was finished, but that still remained.   The Abbess, though rejoiced at the sweet spiritual light shining from the uplifted face of the

The Annunciation.

Virgin, even more glad to see how devotional
Fra Lippi was growing, and how sad the earn-
est look in his eyes became when he had spent
a discouraging day, nevertheless began to
feel a little impatient for the completion of
the altar-piece.

Her life was a busy one with its round of
cares, and she felt that she could hardly spare
so many more hours. The days were fast
approaching when the most sacred relic of
Prato, the Cintola would be shown, and she
must finish the embroidery on the altar-cloth
before that. She had not allowed the nuns to
be present in the chapel during the painting,
so her own work had seemed very little.
Then, too, there were paintings yet waiting
for Fra Lippo to finish at the Cathedral. She
really must speak to him about hastening his
task.

"My brother," she began, but at that
moment a knock on the door interrupted her.
It was Sister Frances, who came to tell the
Abbess that a poor sick beggar had called
and would not be put off, but begged to see

the Abbess, weeping and calling upon the
saints, so Sister Frances had come. The
Abbess looked at Fra Lippi, but he was
absorbed in painting a look of ineffable tenderness about the lips of the Virgin ; she
looked at Lucrezia, but she was staring in an
abstracted sort of way over the door where
texts of the holy writ were illuminated in such
brilliant colors and rich designs ; she looked
helplessly at Sister Frances,—there seemed no
other way. She would be gone only a moment,—and the chapel door closed behind her.

Fra Lippi laid down his brush, then stepped
quickly to Lucrezia's side. Such liquid eyes,
such glistening red-gold hair, such curved red
lips he had never seen—no, not in any of the
cities of Italy. The rosary fell from her hand.
He picked it up, and dropped it into her lap,
murmuring " Lucrezia" ; she could not meet
those burning, dark eyes.

" Lucrezia," he repeated, coming nearer and
stooping to look into her downcast face, until
his shoulder almost brushed her hair. She
put her hand to her throat, her bosom heaved

so, and her white robe became unclasped. Fra Lippi gently took her hands from her neck, and tried to fasten the clasp.

"Lucrezia,"—his speech was the softest murmur, and the dark beautiful eyes so near her own were looking down at her with idolatrous tenderness,—but there were footsteps sounding outside, and she tremulously pushed him away.

When the Abbess entered the chapel, Fra Lippi was painting the Virgin's lips a very rich carmine, while the model, instead of looking abstractedly at the arabesques, was nervously fingering her rosary. The pink tints had faded from her face, and if the Abbess had looked deeper into her eyes she would have seen that tears were not far off.

That night it was impossible for Lucrezia to pray, impossible to think. Her heart was full of dreams, yet soreness. She walked to the window and laid her head on the sill; the night air cooled her flushed cheeks. But she was restless there. She walked through the halls, she came to the chapel door and

paused to listen.   There was no sound.   She
opened the door ; she could see nothing but
the wax taper burning under the cupola of the
altar.   She passed in and went down the nave
behind the altar-screen, not daring even to
look at the Virgin, and sat down before the
organ, and began to play softly.   Soon the
chapel was filled with music, which rose sur-
ging in waves only to die away in low love-
chords.   She felt a draught and saw one of
the windows open.

" Lucrezia ! "—her name was spoken in the
gentlest tones, but it sent the blood to her
heart.

Fra Lippi had entered the chapel so softly
that she had not heard him ; there he stood
before her, dressed in the richness and beauty
of a Florentine noble.   Only once before had
she ever seen him without his monk's robe,—
that night at the Grand Duke's house.

A mantle of deep-red velvet fell from his
shoulder, showing a gold-colored, gold-embroidered satin doublet ; a long white plume
drooped from his cap, and was held in place

by a diamond pin—the recent gift from Cosmo de Medici ; it sparkled like a star in the night. Soft lace encircled his wrists and fell over his handsomely moulded hands. He had carelessly thrown aside the long priest's cloak and hood, by which he had disguised himself.

" Tell me thou lovest me ! " he cried impetuously, taking her hand.

Love him—oh, Mother of God ! what should she do ? Before this she had been happy in the convent, and it had seemed to her the fulness of life—the diurnal prayer periods, the embroidering of altar-cloths, the sacred gifts, the care of the shrine, the making the tapers, the mixing of drugs for the sick, giving bread to beggars, preparing conserves ; but now,—with those eyes so near her own, and the music of his voice repeating :

" Lucrezia, thou lovest me ; Lucrezia, tell me so ! Do not turn away, my beloved—my frightened bird——"

But what if the Abbess should come ? she must think—she must not stay—

" Go ! go ! " she implored.

"To-morrow," he said, as he drew her to him, kissing her again and again. "To-morrow! But how few to-morrows are left! *Cara mia*, the picture is finished, was finished days ago, but for your sweet face which has kept me here!" She clung about his neck a moment. He kissed her hair, her throat.

"Only a few more days at the most—*eh, Dio !*—if I could brush out at night what I have painted in the day—that was a merry example Penelope of old set to a waiting lover,—but I see the Abbess grows impatient. Oh, my Lucrezia !" he cried, drawing her closer to him, " if I could but take you away from here—away with me ; look up, my sweet! This cold dark convent is no place to bury so much light and love, believe me. I spent my boyhood in the Carmine," and he shivered at the memory ; " I know the convents, I know the world,—but with me, Lucrezia, Lucrezia," he whispered.

She hid her head in his breast ; he tried to lift her face, but she clung the closer. Where

were his vows,—where were hers, those she
was to take so soon, those which would separate her from the world with rites of such
awful solemnity?

"My child," he said, knowing her thoughts,
"you cannot shut the world behind you when
you close the convent door upon it; you know
full well that worldliness and corruption are
not all outside the Vatican; you know that
the gentlest men and women are not all found
in convents; you know that the Church on
earth is not all your fond ideals have painted
it; you know that cruelty and indecency,
the intrigues of popes and cardinals are so
well known in Florence that they are jested
at—I do not waken you from a sweet
dream?" he asked, looking down into her
frightened face.

"Oh, Lucrezia, thou art mine—mine! my
loved one, look into my eyes, see my great
love for you!"

A door creaked.

"Go!" she cried, pushing him away; and
in an instant she was alone. It seemed to

8

her that all the light of the chapel was gone,
and the darkness was heavy. She laid her
head on the organ.

" My daughter," said the Abbess, close by
her side, " I thought I heard voices."

Lucrezia started, but in the dim light the
Abbess could not see how pale she was.

" I came in here," she faltered, and stood
looking at the altar. The Abbess misunderstood.

" Ah, my child, you have been here to pray.
As the holy time approaches when you shall
take your vows, you cannot come too often
and prostrate yourself before the shrine of
the blessed Virgin."

A quick blush overspread Lucrezia's face.

" I will leave you, my daughter, to your
meditations. To-morrow Father Antonio will
be here to confession."

Lucrezia trembled. What had she done?
What was she doing? Meet her confessor!
No! Her terrible guilt overwhelmed her.
She could yet see the dark eyes of Lippi
looking into hers, she could feel the beautiful

face so near her cheek, she could hear the
caressing murmurs of his voice.

" O Saint Margaret !" she cried, falling on
her knees before a little image of the convent
saint. " O sweet Saint Margaret ! pity
me, thou who wast led through love to sorrow; pray for me that I may be brought from
this grievous sin !" Yet as she prayed her
heart seemed running over with wild dreams.

" Dost thou love me?" she heard Fra Lippi
whispering.

Love him ! Love him ! The very chancel
seemed full of his presence, while without,
where the *lucciola* burned, she could hear a
nightingale singing of love.

" Tell me thou lovest me !" she heard him
saying. Love him ! tell him she loved him !
Ah, he knew it full well !

" *The picture is already finished !* " Eh,
Dio ! The dreariness of Santa Margharita's
after he should come no more ! Ah, that
wild pain in her heart, which almost stopped
its beating, then sent the blood madly through
her veins ! He was hers, monk though he

was—she was his! The world might crush
her, grind her to the very dust; the Pope
might excommunicate them—no, *her*, but not
her beloved! She shivered as her thoughts re-
coiled, and she remembered how she trembled
before that great fresco of Orcagna,—that
picturing of the judgment-day on the walls of
the Campo Santa. There were not only men
and women of the world, but popes and
monks in torment; if God should smite him—
her Filippo—he had taken such vows—ah,
no! That great splendid soul should never
be lost for her; but she, what mattered it?
She would cast her fears to the winds, every
thing to lie on his breast and clasp his fair
neck in her arms.

"My Filippo! Oh, my Filippo!" she whispered.

The waxed taper flickered and burned out.
The convent was utterly dark. She put out
her hand and instinctively groped about in
the gloom, until she stood before the high
altar, then she threw herself down at the feet
of the Madonna which the dear hand had

painted. She remained motionless, scarcely breathing, until the east became flushed with red, and the morning light touched the borders of the woods; then the sound of the matin bell aroused her and she started up, dazed to see a streak of sunlight coming in through the eastern window.

X.

HE Princess Beatrice walked rest-lessly about her room in Florence pausing now and then before a painting which stood on an easel; over one corner of the carved gilt frame an exquisitely embroidered Eastern scarf was thrown and hung in graceful lines. The picture seemed to intensify the Princess' unrest. It was only a woman's por-trait. Her gown is of deep red velvet, open at the throat and breast, and against the fair, white skin a red rose burns; so much color seems only to heighten the brightness of the face. How the picture glows,—the lips, the cheeks, even in the eyes, are smouldering fires. There was no answering smile on the Princess' face.

118

She walked to the window, and looked down upon the marble blocks in the court-yard below. The air, sweet with the breath of violets, enticed her; she went through the wide halls to the *loggia* and leaned against one of the marble pillars. Everywhere was the voice of water; the swaying noise of the great jet that rose in silvery spray and fell into a wide basin, which had soothed her many times before in her restlessness, only the more vividly brought to memory the unhappiness she strove to forget.

It had been months since she had seen him, that handsome painter from the Carmine; she smiled as she thought of his cowl and gown. He was a very charming monk. What could have kept him from her so long! She knew that he was not in Florence, that went without saying; she wondered if he longed to be at her side again. How well she remem-bered the morning she first saw him. She was sitting with her Uncle Giovanni, in the beautiful Medici gardens, when they saw a monk coming toward them.

" It is Filippo Lippi," said her uncle; " I have sent for him to paint a picture for the King of Naples," and he rose to meet the artist.

He was a monk; before this monks had never interested her, but the name of this one was familiar through stories, told by court ladies, of some most delightfully amusing intrigues. She watched him as her uncle talked with him. Fra Lippi had taken off his small monk's cap, and his dark curls framed his handsome face. The Princess remembered how often his glance wandered to her. She knew perfectly well that she was charming enough to attract an artist's eye, even though he were a monk.

The next day she sent a messenger to summon him to her apartments. He came, and when he looked into her eyes and smiled, the room seemed flooded with sunlight. She asked him to paint her portrait. He came each day just the same after the picture was finished.

Ah! how many times he had kissed her full red lips, and praised her exquisite face. Her beauty intoxicated him. Could it be possible that there was some other face as fair to him, so that she held him enchanted no longer? It was a thought that made the Princess pale a little; not but there might be other men quite as adorable, men not fettered by a brown gown and white mantle.

She walked up and down the *loggia.* Under her feet was a cool mosaic pavement; above her head cherubs were sporting on billowy clouds. How gayly they smiled down at her. She remembered how often Lippo had paced back and forth here, in his impatience for her to join him. Then she would come in some trailing robe, with fleecy lace about her head and shoulders; she wore no jewels around her throat, for Lippo liked it better so,—only a diamond star glistened in the coils of her dusky hair. How eagerly he clasped her to his heart,—then they would go strolling through the gardens; sometimes Lippo would fasten a rose on her breast, and kiss the lips smiling down upon it, then he would put his arm around her and lead her to the seat near

the water which fell over the marble steps.
She could hear it rippling now !

She should think his work in Prato would
be finished.   That was such a dull town ; how
he must long for bright, beautiful Florence.
Prato ! why had she not thought of it before ?
how stupid !   Prato, the very place where
her cousin Lucrezia Buti had gone to escape
a marriage with Senor Aletri.   A richer
radiance overspread the dark face of the
Princess ; she would visit Prato ; who knew
but that she would be blessed with a sight of
Filippo.

She summoned her attendants, ordered her
litter, and was soon beyond the Porta al
Prato.   In her impatience it was a slow, tiresome journey, and the hours passed wearily
until she stood at the heavy convent gate,
seeking admittance.

"Tell your Abbess," she said to the bent,
old servant who answered the call, "that the
Princess Beatrice of Florence desires to see
her cousin, Lucrezia Buti."   The old portress
had not seen such flashing jewels and rich

brocades since she served in the ducal palace at Arezzo ; the beauty of the woman, too, quite dazzled her. She showed the Princess to the Abbess' room with a deferential air given to only the Archbishop himself.

She soon returned saying that the Abbess could not see her until noon ; she was in the chapel, which was being decorated by a painter from the Carmine.

"From the Carmine," repeated the Princess, stopping the old woman, who had turned to go out ; "what is the painter's name?" then added carelessly, as a suspicious look crossed the face of the servant :

"Is he a famous man?"

"He paints beautiful saints, my lady, or he would not be in the chapel of Santa Margharita."

"Is he tall and dark?" questioned the Princess, slipping a gold piece in the bony hand before her.

"Yes," answered the old woman, softening a little. "His eyes are large and dark, his face is dark too,—yet his smile is so bright that one never trembles before him as before some of the holy fathers."

The Princess turned from her and looked about the room, but there was something so bare, so uninviting to one who had been used to luxury, that she longed for the brightness of the court-yard, and followed the servant out the door.

She paced back and forth under the arcades, busy with her thoughts. She had no doubt but that Lippi was painting in that very chapel. She was near him. How her heart thrilled! She must see him! Would he clasp her to his breast in that impetuous way of old? Her eyes grew brighter, and the red flush burned under the olive hue of her cheeks.

Would the hour never go! How dull a convent was! What could ever possess women to shut themselves in its narrow walls. Yet she knew so many who did—handsome ones, too, who had as many lovers as she. Perhaps, if Filippo were to paint forever in that chapel, she would come here and take the vows of a nun, if only to see him as he passed in and out that door. How unbearable life was becoming, without his cheering voice and careless gayety.

The hour was only half gone now. She stopped beside the fountain, and looked into the water in the stone basin, and saw the reflection of her face. What an exquisite poise, what a curve of the neck!

What could keep the Abbess so long in the chapel—it must be unnecessary. Yet she would not mind being an abbess if she could watch Filippo paint—only she would have to wear such coarse gowns, and cut her beautiful waving hair. After all, there was something picturesque about their lives; she had heard very romantic whisperings about certain great ladies who had entered convents. There were such handsome friars too. But there was Lucrezia Buti. It would be just like her to take religious vows, and lead a saintly life—she was such a simple child, and cared so little about lovers. Well, perhaps she would never have many—how intolerable that must be!

What an hour! but it was almost gone. Perhaps if she should step behind one of those great pillars the Abbess would not see her when she came out, then Filippo would follow her at a distance, and she would stop him —for just a moment,—for just one word.

"Oh, Filippo!" she murmured to herself, as she rested her cheek against the cold stone. The noon bell rang. "Ah!" she exclaimed, and her heart beat so fast it almost suffocated her. The heavy wooden door opposite her, that led to the chapel, opened. The black-robed figure of the Abbess appeared; behind her came a slight, fair girl, in a white trailing gown.

The Princess leaned more heavily against the pillar. It was all so plain to her now— Lucrezia had been in the chapel; Filippo was painting the Virgin from her face. How horrible it all was,—but how foolish her fears were. As soon as the door closed, and the Abbess and the girl were out of sight, Beatrice swiftly

glided along the cloister until she came to the
chapel door, then noiselessly opened it and
closed it behind her. She could see nothing
at first, the sun outside shining on the marble
had been so bright; she lingered a moment
until, in the gloom, she saw a figure standing
before an easel. It was Filippo—the Princess
started forward.

"Filippo," she softly breathed, "Filippo,
you have long been absent from me."

Fra Lippi turned and saw the Princess
Beatrice before him. He started a little, then
gallantly kissed her hand, saying:

"It is my unhappiness that I have been
kept from Florence"; but there was an in-
sincere undertone in what he said—he had
never spoken to her in this way before.

She proudly drew herself up to her full
height, and said, looking at the picture:

"You are painting Madonnas from a model."
Then added insinuatingly, "This is very good
of my cousin, yet I dare say that Senor Buti
did not place his daughter here for just this
purpose."

"You do not alarm me," he interrupted. "I have the Abbess' consent as well as Father Antonio's."

"The Abbess' consent," she repeated scornfully, "pray, what does an Abbess in Prato know about——" but she dared go no further. Something in Fra Lippi's face stopped her, and she assumed the pleading rôle.

"Filippo," she said softly, placing her hand on his arm, "I have missed you, have you not thought of me?"—but no gentler expression came to his lips.

The Princess had seen enough of men to know that she no longer had power over Lippi. A look of hatred gleamed in her eyes, and without a word she turned and swept out of the chapel. She went directly to the Abbess' door and rapped. The Abbess opened it, and looked at Beatrice with a gentle smile; "I was told you were here," she said.

"I was tired with the journey," faltered the Princess, "so I sought the court-yard; I came to visit Lucrezia, my cousin, for a few hours. When I arrived I could not see her," she went on, looking directly at the Abbess, who flushed a little, but bravely said :

" Lucrezia was performing a sacred duty."

" Ah !" said the Princess ; she was deciding just how she could prejudice this unsophisticated woman against Fra Lippi. But the Abbess dismissed the conversation by saying: " Lucrezia is now in her room, you may see her there."

9

XI.

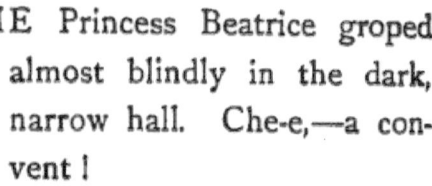HE Princess Beatrice groped almost blindly in the dark, narrow hall. Che-e,—a convent !

Why had she not come here, to Santa Margharita's, before ! She had known that Filippo was in Prato—she could have easily found out that he was painting in the convent chapel. She would have seen him someway, even if she could not pose for a Madonna.

" Oh, Filippo, Filippo !" she cried, sinking down upon the step at the head of the stairs. "Oh, Filippo ! If I were a weaker woman, my heart would have broken when you looked at me so in the chapel ! "

If she only could have known sooner how easily she could have persuaded Senor Buti to insist upon Lucrezia's marriage. If she could have known ! It might not be too late now—Guido Aletri's palace would be as secure a shelter as a convent—the Senor a better guard than an Abbess. She started to her feet—Lucrezia had not the spirit to brave her ;—oh, Filippo was cruel !

She found the door of Lucrezia's room : she listened a moment, then, after softly knocking, opened the door and entered.

Lucrezia was standing in front of her little crucifix. She had not yet taken off her white gown, but seemed to be half-dreaming. She started when she heard footsteps, then went hurriedly forward to welcome her Cousin Beatrice.

" How good you are to come to see me," she said, then stopped suddenly when she looked at the Princess, who seemed to be mastering some intense emotion. Her breath came short, her jewels sparkled, rising and falling on her bosom with each heart-throb.

Lucrezia had never seen her look lovelier. Her dark hair was drawn from her low brow and fastened in a large coil at the back of her neck. Her face was half shaded by the wide hat and drooping plumes. Lucrezia saw the Princess gazing in a surprised way at her own light gown, and then at the black novice robe which was thrown across the chair. She flushed, and stood embarrassed, waiting for her cousin to speak.

Beatrice came forward and kissed Lucrezia's cheek, saying: "I came to see how you were enjoying these weeks of convent life."

The color burned deeper in Lucrezia's face, and she stood awkwardly, yet resenting the sharp glance of the Princess.

"You are decked in court robes," she said.

Lucrezia still could say nothing.

"Perhaps you would like to return with me? Your wedding gown—as well as Senor Aletri—is still waiting for you."

"Oh, no!" cried Lucrezia, with a shudder. "I am going to stay here—I am going to take the vows," the Princess drew a breath of re-

lief. It was better so—far safer. The painting was almost done. When once Filippo
returned to Florence,—ah, well! The pain
in her breast gave place to hope.

She smiled more softly at Lucrezia. But
then the danger might not be over. That
gown was ravishing in its simplicity. Strange
that she had never noticed the curves of Lucrezia's throat. Her hair too,—it would be
far less likely to ensnare if it were behind the
bandeau.

"Are nuns allowed such finery as this?"
she questioned. "How can you keep your
mind from the things of the world when you
are arrayed in this fashion?" Lucrezia hesitated, and seemed about to speak when the
Princess began again.

" I have been in the chapel—I saw the altar-
piece—I have known Filippo Lippi a long
time—his smile is dangerous. Go to-morrow
in your nun's garb, if you would keep your
heart clean and his soul from peril. It is useless to indulge your vanity longer; the garment of the Virgin is painted, put this in

your chest again,—it is better for your soul, my child."

The Princess walked nervously up and down the little room. It was stifling there. She must be off; it would be nightfall before she reached Florence.

She turned to Lucrezia. "Beware of the soft speeches of men, even though they wear holy robes. I can trust you," she added, as she went out of the door. Lucrezia felt that, in spite of Beatrice's hauteur, there was an unconscious appeal in her manner.

What could her cousin mean? Why had she come to her in this manner and seemed so agitated? It was all so strange to her that she felt bewildered. Could Beatrice suspect, when she said "Beware of soft speeches"? It could not be—surely Beatrice did not suppose she was unaccompanied by the Abbess or a Sister? She spoke of the painting. Fra Lippi must have been in the chapel; had she talked with him, and had he shown her the altar-piece? Then to speak so of her going back to Florence,—and of her gown! As if

the painting concerned the Princess, or as if
caution were necessary! Lucrezia was ready
to break into tears. She walked to the window, crossing herself as she passed the little
crucifix. Several nuns were walking in the
court-yard. She was glad that she said that
about taking the vows. Surely there she was
equal to Beatrice. Perhaps she had perplexed
her. She hoped so. And the nun's garb!
Why had her cousin mentioned that? Did
she think it less becoming? Was she really
jealous?

Lucrezia watched two of the Sisters as they
turned to walk back under the arcade, the
sunshine falling upon them as it found its way
among the columns. She could not but notice, as she had so often done, the peculiar
beauty of the simple robes, the charm of white
and black, the contrast of veil and bandeau.
She knew how frequently some of the Sisters
had spoken of her robe, that it was her true
dress, in it her face was sweetest.

Lucrezia smiled; Beatrice had not seen her
wear it. But should she make the change?

If she did, Beatrice would think her under her power.   But no!   She was not !   She was independent !   Her cousin might draw whatever conclusion she pleased ; she would perplex her still more in the end.   Beatrice deserved it.

But what would Fra Lippi think ?   Ah ! that was the real question.   His face would show.   He would speak.   Could it be that the Sisters were right—was she more beautiful ?   Here was the opportunity for her to know.   She would do it.   The Frate should be the judge.   Yet if he should question it, if he should wish the change, what reason should she give to him ?   Would that not be difficult ?   But she would think of something before the morning.   She would not trouble herself about it now.   And the Abbess ?   She could give some excuse to her too.

It was all solved easier than Lucrezia thought.   She rose from her seat at the window and changed the white gown for the dark one.   Then went to the Abbess' room to embroider as usual.

" Lucrezia," said the Abbess when they
were alone, after the other Sisters who were
working on the altar-cloth had gone, "your
cousin, the Princess, came to me after she left
you. She is very anxious that you return to
Florence. Is it your wish to do so ? "

" No," answered Lucrezia, quietly.

" And you remain with the desire to take
the vows ? "

" That is my reason." The model for the
Madonna might have said more.

The Abbess began to speak of the solemn
duties of consecration. But Lucrezia was
silent. The vesper bell rang. The painting
had not been mentioned that afternoon.

" Are you not ready ? " said the Abbess
next morning when she went to Lucrezia's
room and found her still in her nun's garb.

" Yes."

" But the gown ? "

" I shall not wear it."

For a moment the Abbess seemed surprised, but something occurred to her.

"The dear donzella!" she said to herself,
"it is the vow that she will take. She re-
members it even as a model. But I did not
mean this in my talk last evening. Her
spirit is saintly."

She said nothing to Lucrezia, only "Come,
we will go," and together they entered the
chapel.

It was a great relief to Lucrezia that the
Abbess said no more about the change, yet
she could not help wondering the reason,
as they descended to the court-yard and
approached the chapel. She wondered if Fra
Lippi would like it. She thought of that the
first thing when she awoke; now she began to
feel a little faint-hearted about it. She found
it more difficult than she supposed to think of
excuses; she dreaded the Abbess, but she
had hardly noticed the change. Perhaps Fra
Lippi would not. She had been as foolish as
a child, she impatiently thought, as she remembered how she had taken the white gown
from the chest that morning after mass, how
soft its folds were, how simple its fashion!

She had fallen into a reverie as it lay spread out upon her couch. She had been almost tempted to wear it, yet she hesitated,—how wicked she was growing!

Fra Lippi had officiated at morning mass, and she could now hear the prayers as he intoned them. She knew that the Virgin Mary must listen to that voice when it was uplifted in supplication. Ah! it was more musical and rich than that of any priest she had ever heard—the voice that would so soon speak to her in approval or disappointment.

She thought how long she sat there dreaming, how the time went sooner than she was aware. She heard the Abbess' footsteps on the stairs. Then it was too late. Besides she was resolved, and hastily restored the gown to its place. She wondered what the Abbess was thinking of as she walked so placidly across the court-yard ; in spite of her gentleness Lucrezia knew her heart had suffered its tragedy. But these thoughts were soon absorbed in others. Her heart beat fast as she saw Fra Lippi in the chancel awaiting them.

At first he supposed some Sister was with
the Abbess.   In the dim light he did not recognize Lucrezia.   Could it be that she was not
coming this morning !   Was she ill ?   Yet he
had seen her at mass.   All unconscious as he
seemed of the worshippers, the eyes of the
monk had wandered over the faces of the
kneeling nuns.   The face he sought was there.
The artist as well as priest was at the altar.
The effect of bandeau and veil !   The glance
had impressed the heart more deeply than ever
before.   His beautiful Lucrezia,—why was she
not here ?   Had the Princess made mischief
yesterday—he would call the saints to curse
her !

But this was his beloved now, coming
towards him with the Abbess, and they had
almost reached the chancel railing.   Strange
he should not have known her sooner.   He
was so used to that other gown—he had
never thought of her in a nun's habit.   The
first morning he saw only her face; that night
in the chapel he could only distinguish the
dark, sombre outline, the candle burned so

dim,—but now—her face was all the sweeter in its purity. And this picture had been in his thoughts since he saw it at mass. Now he should have her before him !

" I had almost wondered who accompanied you," said Lippi, smiling and addressing the Abbess as he stepped forward to open the gate. But his eyes were upon Lucrezia.

The blood rushed through her veins. He was not disappointed, he thought her as beautiful, or why should he look so and smile? Lucrezia forgot her beating heart. He was speaking to her as the Abbess stepped forward to look at the painting.

"The other gown? Did you know how near the picture is finished ? "

Why had she not thought of this before ? Had not Beatrice told her so, when she spoke of seeing the picture?

"Yes," said Lucrezia softly, and blushed. She sank into the chair, her upturned face looking into Lippi's. He drew nearer. The light from his eyes seemed to flash sunshine through her. He was standing

bending over her, the left hand with the
palette upon the chair. She did not turn
away her head, but smiled gently. The Abbess was still behind the easel looking at the
painting. With a quick movement Filippo
stooped down, his lips lightly brushed Lucrezia's brow.

" My beloved! my heart's love! never before
so beautiful!" he murmured. The mantle fell
from his shoulders, and he stood in his cour-
tier's dress. In a moment the cloak was drawn
about him, and he was again at the Abbess'
side.

Fra Filippo Lippi and Lucrezia Buti

Castagnola

XII.

HE last day of the painting had come. Fra Lippi could not prolong the work. It was absolutely finished, and the panel placed above the altar. The Abbess walked down the nave, to stand near the door of the chapel to look at the altar-piece from that distance. The transfigured form of the Virgin was borne upward in a radiant flood of golden light; a glow of celestial rapture was diffused over all. Here was spotless grace, given with a depth of expression that surprised the Abbess.

Before this she had felt that it was only the intensely human character which appealed to Lippi, and, although this did not wholly sat-

isfy or realize her spiritual conception of the
Virgin, there was a freshness and devotion of
feeling that put to shame the sanctification of
glitter and embroidered robes and jewelled
crowns of the latter-day saints and Madonnas.
The sublime expression on the sweet girlish
face was striking; Fra Lippi had endued the
immortal woman with life and light—yes, with
even deity. With almost a girlish gesture,
the girdle was dropped into the outstretched
arms of St. Thomas; the tomb was filled
with flowers,—earth and its sorrows were left
below.

While the Abbess stood serenely gazing
into the beautiful uplifted face of the Virgin,
her thoughts went back over the past, and
she looked longer than she had any idea.
Lucrezia sat pale and silent. Fra Lippi
stepped about gathering up his brushes. He
drew near Lucrezia.

"To-night," he whispered, "I am coming
to thee.—Be here as before, my darling—I
have missed the light in thy smile, my Lucrezia! But to-night——"

The Abbess came slowly down the nave. Her eyes were full of tears, but the expression of her face told Fra Lippi that she was more than glad she had consented to the waiting and delay.

.   .   .   .

The sun went down, and the sky was filled with a rosy light that flushed the city with radiance. Lucrezia leaned out of her window and heard the bells of Florence tolling. The music filled the air ; then she knew that in the churches hundreds of voices were chanting the Ave Maria. She tried to worship in accord, and hush the anxiety of her heart by prayer. Twilight faded, and she could see only dark shadows where so short a time ago sunlight had tinted the distant hills. The sound of the fountain came clear to her in the intense stillness, and she heard a nightingale singing in the orange-trees. In the moonlight the roses were nodding one above the other ; farther in the shade she could see the *lucciola*, in whose heart was hidden the love words caught from lovers' lips—what

10

a mission for a flower! As if one could forget,—in her heart were treasured those sweetest, tenderest words, too dear to die, too precious to be trusted even to a flower.

She walked restlessly up and down. The bell in Santo Stefano struck. It was almost the time that Fra Lippi was coming. She felt no power to resist, she only knew that she loved. She opened the chapel door, then walked to one window, then the other, to listen. Her light footsteps sounded heavy on the cold stone. At last she fancied she heard the tramp of horses' feet,—but her heart beat so loudly she could hardly listen ; she peered through the darkness but all was still, —so still the only sound she heard was the beating of her heart. Ah! yes, the sound of hoofs came nearer, then stopped—she strained her ear to listen—at that moment the chapel door opened and the Abbess came in.

Lucrezia stepped back in the shadow of the pillar, scarcely breathing. She heard the chancel gate clang, then one flame after another burned from the candles on the altar. She watched the flickering lights, and stood expecting every moment to hear the window lightly raised. The Abbess came down the nave—she saw Lucrezia.

" For whom dost thou wait ? " she asked, a little suspiciously. " Art thou ready for the confessional ? Father Antonio is here."

With a low cry Lucrezia sank down—she heard the notes of the grilli outside—Filippo was there—O Blessed Mary, pity, pity !

Fra Lippi walked impatiently up and down by the convent wall until the gray dawn made him hasten away,—but no note in answer came to his call.

XIII.

HE days dragged on. Lucrezia grew pale and listless; the pain and penance attending her vows wore upon her. In place of the gentle happiness, shining in her eyes there came a deep troubled look, which reminded the Abbess of Fra Angelico's Virgin of Sorrows. The rose flush had faded from her cheeks, her lips had lost the childish curves. The weight in her heart grew heavier; she felt herself the most abandoned of human beings. Such a love as hers would burn her soul to all eternity; she could not tear it from her heart with fasting or with prayers, and she dared not tell her confessor. To-morrow she was to take the solemn vows of a nun for that life which, in the confusing, flaring light of Florence with its rush of intrigues, its glitter and hollowness, had seemed the opened door of peace. The love-making of the rich old noble, Guido Aletri, had been to her the most uncomfortable thing in the world, from which she should escape. Her father had urged her strongly to the marriage, her aunt had already her wedding finery prepared. She had been so happy the first weeks in the convent—but now it had all changed.

She wondered where Fra Lippi was,—she was never to see him again,—there could be no way. She was never to think of him— God help her ! She looked out her little window to the slope on either side, covered with vineyards. The fruit hung heavy in rich clusters, but the vine dressers that had been so busy had left their work and were coming in groups to Santo Stefano, where to-day the most sacred relic, the Cintola of the Virgin was to be shown. The nuns of the convent were to go in solemn procession. She already heard the Abbess' voice in the hall. She must hasten.

If only the sight of the girdle could miraculously soothe the pain in her heart, if it could take away the bitter memory of the past months, if it could bring peace—she trembled lest she had lost her sweet childish faith in the power of the blessed relic. But she would go with the others, she would try to worship, even though she knew that the sight of the girdle would bring to her more vividly than any thing else the days in the chapel while Fra Lippi was painting her as the Madonna Cintola. This very morning, when the nuns had assembled in the Abbess' room after early mass, to hear the sacred legends, she had lived over in that time the fierce sorrows of the last few months. It seemed as if the Abbess' story would never come to an end—it was so stifling there—may the Virgin forgive her impiety! —she could hear again the gentle monotone of the Abbess as she said:

" When the blessed Virgin rose from the tomb, and in sight of the Apostles ascended into glory, the Apostle St. Thomas was absent; after three days he returned, but doubted the truth of her glorious assumption. The tomb was opened, that he might believe, and lo! it was found empty! The ever gracious Mother, pitying his weakness and want of faith, appeared to him in a vision and dropped her girdle into his hand, that all doubt should be forever removed from his mind. Since that day the churches of the West and East had striven to possess that sacred treasure. Through a thousand years it had been miraculously preserved. Then when Michael Dogomari of Prato, after the crusade of 1096 was over, travelled through Eastern lands, and by grace of the holy Virgin came to Jerusalem, he lodged in a house of a Greek priest, to whom the care of the sacred relic had descended. To his daughter, whom he loved passing well, he entrusted the keeping of the girdle. Michael staying in the house, and seeing the beautiful maid, became enamoured, and unable to gain the consent of the priest to their marriage, went to the mother. The daughter's tears and love so moved the mother's heart that she consented to their union, still entrusting the girdle to the daughter's keeping, and assisted the lovers in their flight. The voyage from the Holy Land to the shores of Tuscany was most calm, which the mariners attributed to the power of the sacred relic.

" Michael, with the precious casket in his hand and his bride by his side, disembarked at Pisa, and came to his home at Prato. There guardian angels attended him, in spite of which Michael, so jealous of his treasure and fearful of being robbed, lighted a lamp every night and placed the casket under his bed. This lack of faith so offended the guardian angels that every night they lifted him from his bed and placed him on the bare earth, which sore affliction he endured rather than risk the loss of his treasure. When growing old, the pious Michael fell sick and died, but on his death-bed gave the sacred girdle to the Bishop Uberto, who promised to preserve it in the Cathedral, and from time to time present it for the worship of the people.

"It was carried in solemn procession by torch-bearing priests to Santo Stefano, where it will be shown to you this morning. What wonder that the people of Prato venerate this precious relic! What wonder that they put to death that impious traitor Musciatino, who attempted to rob the church of its treasure! What wonder that they showed their appreciation by building that inviolable shrine! Go to your rooms and spend a half-hour in praise and devotion. Prepare your hearts for any miracle the Virgin may choose to perform through the blessed agency of the Cintola."

When the nuns drew near the Cathedral they found the space around the entrance crowded, and the people were jostling and pushing one another that each might stand nearer the open-air pulpit, from which the priest would show the relic. In the church the Brotherhood were chanting. As the moments passed the crowd grew more impatient and pressed nearer the sacred object. A cripple near Lucrezia had vigorously used his crutch that he might prevent others going before him; the poor and the sick looked with expectant eyes, praying for bread for their little ones, and health for themselves; the youths and the maidens awaited no less eagerly the answering of their more joyous requests.

Lucrezia dared not hope or pray, but stood with eyes fixed upon the empty pulpit. There was a movement among those in front, the crowd behind pushed forward—all eyes were upon the priest who stood before them; he was speaking. In the sudden hush that followed, a voice other than that of the holy Father's ravished Lucrezia's ears.

"My beloved! sh— do not start,—to-night, Lucrezia mine, come to the outer gate at midnight. You must, you shall escape!"

Before she could answer, Fra Lippi was lost in the crowd. The priest disappeared with the relic. The people turned to go to their homes. Whatever miraculous things it had wrought to the suppliant worshippers, it had answered an unuttered prayer.

When Fra Lippi stood outside the gate, all was dark and quiet at the convent. He paused and listened, but heard no sound. The moments had been hours, the hours had been days,—it had been an eternity since he had stood by the side of his beloved. What a picture of the Virgin he would paint, now that she had so graciously answered his prayer! It was like a glimpse of paradise, to see the face of his beloved once more! The midnight bell struck. She would soon be here! What a night! how perfect! The hill-sides were hushed, the very leaves were still, the olive woods shone silvery in the moonlight; a delicate odor of spices and fruit and flowers was borne from the fertile meadows that stretch towards Pistoja.

How the moments dragged! where was his dear one—a melancholy, as dark as the brightness of his joy, came over his face,—was she not coming, had any thing happened? Saint Albert! nothing should keep her from him now; he would move heaven and earth. She was his, she loved him—her eyes had told him so! The memory of her sad, pale face had pained him all day. How the color rushed to her cheeks when he spoke to her that morning! She had missed him—his Lucrezia!

A fleecy cloud hid the moon—the lightest footstep sounded on the stone—the bolt was noiselessly drawn.

"Is it thou?" he whispered.

Lucrezia, pale and tremulous, stepped over the sill and closed the gate. Filippo caught her in his arms; she, not accustomed to the darkness, peered into his face. The soft moonlight fell about her. A dark cloak concealed the white gown.

"My beloved!" he cried; but she covered his mouth with her fingers. His clear, vibrating laugh rang out upon the still air; he suddenly checked it. "I did not know where I was—I thought I was in *Paradiso!*" he said, his lips still laughing.

Lucrezia drew a deep breath. All the pain and weariness were gone, she was with her lover!

"Lucrezia! Lucrezia!" he cried, pressing

his face close upon hers. "*Dio!* what an Inferno Florence has been these last weeks. I thought I was never to look upon this divine face—oh, my angel! my blessed one!"

With his arm yet around her waist, Filippo led her down the slope, where, in the shadow of the mulberry trees, two horses were waiting. A figure stepped from the shade, and gave the bridles to Lippi. Lucrezia saw it was a monk, and recognized him as Fra Diamante, the Carmelite who came to the chapel one morning while Filippo was painting the altar-piece.

Fra Diamante quickly disappeared—then all she could remember was clattering along the streets, turning sharp corners, riding under low arcades, through narrow passages, until they came to the open way, and Prato was left behind. As the morning star twinkled in the sky, the city of Florence lay before them; the old gray walls of convents and palaces began to take on a radiance from the east; the Duomo, crowned by the genius of Brunelleschi, rose among the crowd of towers, while by its side, white and stately, stood the Campanile of Giotto. Fra Lippi silently reined in his horse, and came nearer Lucrezia. They both stopped, and looked before them.

" My beloved, the convent is behind; life and love await," he said, gently kissing her fair cheek.

XIV.

HE Abbess missed Lucrezia at early mass the next morning. She wondered what could have kept her this morning of all mornings,— she must be ill; she went to her room and rapped on the door. There was no answer. She rapped louder, then listened, but heard no sound. She opened the door, Lucrezia was not there. The room was just as she had left it the night before. Her black nun's robe was lying across the couch,—the white gown was not in the little chest which Lucrezia had left. The Abbess hastened down-stairs, through the court-yard, to the orchard, then back to the chapel, but there was no trace of the missing novice. A thought came to the Abbess—it was yet early morning,—she crossed the courtyard and came to the heavy wooden door; it was closed, but the bolt was drawn from the inside.

The Abbess stood as if stunned. Lucrezia was gone! Could it be that she had fled? On the very morning she was to have taken the vows! The Abbess could not account for it. There could be no reason. Lucrezia had seemed so happy,—yet had she been happy? The Abbess remembered, now that she thought of it, that Lucrezia had grown a little more pale and silent, but that, until now, had seemed to the Abbess a natural result of penance and night prayers preparatory to taking her vows.

She walked back to her room, saying nothing to the Sisters about Lucrezia's absence and her anxiety, wondering what Father Antonio would say. He would be there very soon. Indeed an hour had hardly gone before she heard his voice in the refectory. It was earlier than she expected. She nervously clasped her rosary and prepared to meet him. As he entered the room she noticed that in place of his usual calm expression there was a troubled look upon his face, which echoed the anxiety at her heart.

"I have been waiting for you, Father," said the Abbess, "and longed to see you."

"I can tell you the cause of your trouble," he replied quietly. "Already the news has reached me. Lucrezia left the convent with Fra Lippi—they are in Florence."

The color slowly left the Abbess' cheeks, and she leaned heavily against the chair.

"At the early dawn this morning," continued Father Antonio, motioning for the Abbess to be seated, "Brother Giovanni went from the San Marco to administer extreme unction to a dying man just beyond the Porta al Prato. When he came from the cottage, he heard the clatter of hoofs, then saw two horses with their riders come down the road. They stopped near the house, and without thinking, he stood in the shadow and watched them. He saw that it was a man and young

11

woman, and was about to pass on when he heard them talking and recognized the voice of Filippo Lippi. 'Do not be alarmed, my dear one,' he said, 'the convent of Santa Margharita is far behind—you are with me!' Then he guided his horse still nearer that of his companion, and taking her hand in his began to speak in lower tones. Brother Giovanni heard the girl say : ' I can almost see the walls of my father's palace—we are so near—I am terrified.' Fra Lippi seemed to be reassuring her, Giovanni occasionally caught fragments of sentences, and heard Lippi say *'Lucrezia,'* then he kissed her and they rode on. Brother Giovanni hurriedly came back to the convent, and aroused me." The look of pain on Father Antonio's face deepened. "We went immediately to Fra Lippi's house, but it was too late ; he answered my call, but defied me. I could not see Lucrezia ; then I sought Senor Buti, but he was in Venice. My dear Abbess," he continued, pacing the floor, "you must go back with me immediately to find Lucrezia and bring her back to this holy place."

"I will be ready straightway," she said, and hastened to her room.

There was no time to be lost; yet she longed to sit down and think. It was so incredible that such a thing could have happened in these walls before her very face, and she be so ignorant of it. She was grieved, she was horrified. She wished she had opposed more strongly Fra Lippi's coming to the convent. Had she not felt that it would bring evil? Yet when he came, his smile, his manner, quite disarmed her; she liked him, she trusted him. Why should she think he would ever prove himself so base. The whispers and rumors were indeed true. She hated him now! Who could ever trust a Florentine! And Lucrezia Buti! gentle, lovely Lucrezia, who at this very hour would have been a holy nun!

The Abbess stood beside her window and looked towards the beautiful flower-like city, in which she had not set foot during these last ten years. She was to ride by the very villa where she lived when a child—by the very almond-tree where she met her lover.

Ah ! love !   Lucrezia was young !

Love ! every one must have one's own experience—but this was all so shocking. She hastily wiped away the tears and went down-stairs.

" I am ready," she calmly said to Father Antonio.

He little guessed the awakened memories, the struggle in her breast, or realized how gently she thought of Lucrezia.

It was a silent journey to Florence. Over the whole Val d'Arno there was a flood of sunlight. She watched the outline of the spires and domes as they approached the city. The surrounding hill-sides were scarlet and purple, gold and bronze, with now and then great masses of green where ilex trees and acanthus grew. The wine pressers were shouting gayly. There were so much light and life in the world, the Abbess felt almost as if she had lost them in the shadow of the convent.

Even as they rode through the streets of Florence the Abbess took little notice of the changes that had taken place since she was there. About the Duomo crowds came and went. She heard the ringing hammers of the carpenters, as they sounded from many an unfinished mass of buildings. In the shops of the goldsmiths and mosaic-makers, apprentices were learning the trade ; men were buying and selling dainty gold and silver garlands. Now and then the note of a mandolin was heard. All was life, mirth, and tumult. How fair was the city, the city that seemed to be girt only by lilies,—but the stones were dark with blood. Why was there so much beauty and fragrance about it? Had it no conscience? The Abbess thought it was like a flower-crowned maiden, with a smile on her lips but more sadness in her eyes than lies in tears. Ah ! the day was not far off when the blossomed crown would be snatched from her hair, and she would sit in sackcloth, with ashes on her head ! But now everywhere were songs and rills of laughter !

They came to Fra Lippi's house, but it had a deserted, empty appearance.

"It is as I feared," said Father Antonio, "they are not here."

They turned their horses towards the Porta al Prato.

Beyond the gate, how serene, how divinely restful the convent, on its quiet hill-side, looked.

XV.

OME of the holy fathers wished the Madonna Cintola taken down from the high altar, since through it such disgrace had come to the convent. But the Abbess, in spite of her unwillingness in the first place to have the chapel adorned, and her objections to the artist the fathers had chosen, was opposed to having the altar-piece removed. Father Antonio granted her wish. So Lucrezia's face was ever before the Abbess in the chapel, and not even for a day had it been allowed her to forget the unhappy affair.

In all this time the Abbess had not seen Lucrezia, and three years had gone by. She heard that all the attempts of Senor Buti to bring Lucrezia home were in vain. She would not leave Filippo. There must be some grace in him that one so pure, so beautiful, should forsake all and cling to him. There must be something deeper than that charm of manner which had attracted the Abbess from the very first. Under the blithesome, light-hearted exterior a soul must be hidden, or Lucrezia would never love him; for love is not blind, love sees, as well as forgives. She heard that Fra Lippi was painting Madonnas more beautiful than ever, and angels with crisp curling hair like the baby Filippino's. Yes; Fra Lippi was once again in Prato, finishing his frescos begun three years ago in the Cathedral.

The Abbess longed to see Lucrezia, and one beautiful day in the spring she stood at the door of Fra Lippi's house.

"You need not announce my name," she said to the maid who answered her knock, "I am sure your mistress will see me." The girl, knowing nothing of Lucrezia's past, took the

Abbess to her apartments. Lucrezia started when she saw who stood before her.

"My dear," said the Abbess, " I have wished to see you many times—why were you so long hidden from us ? " A quick blush overspread Lucrezia's face. "I have not sought you to reproach you," continued the Abbess. " We missed you at the convent ; we wanted you with us ; but if you could not be happy there," —the Abbess hesitated and smiled sadly,— "are you happy now, my child ? "

Lucrezia did not answer for a moment.

" The convent is open to you," the Abbess continued, but Lucrezia only drew Filippino the closer to her breast, and shook her head.

"My father has cast me off," she said, "which makes me very unhappy ; Filippo is away through the day, which makes me lonely ; but when he comes at night, then I smile again."

The Abbess saw that Lucrezia had grown older during these years, but she was more beautiful than ever—a deeper, maturer loveliness that would still increase.

"Come to me again," said Lucrezia as the Abbess rose to go. "I have thought of you so often, and many, many times wished to see you. I knew you would be kind to me." She faltered. "People make me so wretched ; you know that my old friends in Florence never spoke to me if they met me in the Piazza,—so I did not go out often."

The Abbess' heart was deeply touched. She longed to take this sweet child back to the sheltering walls of Santa Margharita's. She would never pain Lucrezia's innocent soul by even hinting that the gay ladies who passed her by only too gladly welcomed Fra Lippi to their houses in the years before.

Ah ! poor child ! poor Lucrezia !

The Abbess gently kissed her and went back to the convent. She often visited Lucrezia, but it was in the hours she knew Fra Lippi was at the Cathedral. She could not see him ; she had not quite forgiven him ; but Lucrezia,—it was somewhat different with her.

Lucrezia was happier in Prato than in

Florence, yet even here her sensitive soul was wounded by cold looks and suggestive shrugs of shoulders. She saw less and less of her beloved Filippo, and she felt a good deal of heart-ache in the midst of her love. Not that Filippo caused it—his caresses had never been tenderer,—but she was alone so much. Sometimes the tears would almost come to her eyes when she timidly asked if he were going out that evening. But when he told her he was tired of four walls after being shut up in them all day long with his brush and his colors, she could not reproach him; still there was a sore spot in her breast that his playful kiss and charming, light-hearted smile could not take away.

The quiet was not disagreeable, even though before this her life had been in the midst of Florentine gayety. She did not wish it now; but the long evenings were so dreary! She would hold the sleeping Filippino in her arms, trying to soften her grief, and think she was glad that Filippo could find rest with his companions after the long day of confinement in the Cathedral. She would put aside her own selfish disappointment in the solitary hours,— Filippo was always so good to her. Dear Filippo! His footsteps sounded outside. He saw through the open blind Lucrezia looking down with adoration into the little upturned, smiling face of Filippino. How beautiful, how even childish were the curves and dimples of her face, how the maternal love-light shone in her eyes, how sweet was the purity of her features!

"Ah, do not move, Lucrezia *mia!*" he exclaimed; "you are now the *Madre Pia!* I shall carry that sweet scene in my heart, and some time give it to the world!" How happy she was then! How quickly heavy hearts grow light!

The next day he came home earlier than usual. "Lucrezia, *carina*," he said, taking her in his arms, "I must leave you for a little. Benedetto Buonfigli has sent for me to come to Perugia—it will be for only a few weeks, my sweet, then I come back again to still labor in the Cathedral. Where is the *bam-*

bino ? " he asked. "Oh, here you are, with a pencil so soon, too—that is right, little one, you will paint great pictures some day. You must be good to your *Madre*—do not cry, pretty one, while I am away." He tossed Filippino in his arms, kissed his chubby cheeks, turned again to Lucrezia, and stroked her shining hair.

" You are as beautiful as ever, my beloved, even more lovely than when I first lost my heart to you. It has been a very true heart since then—smile, my Lucrezia—do not let me take with me the memory of tears ; you must not let the color go from your cheeks ; you must always be beautiful for me—my inspiration ! Without your dear face before me, how could I paint a Madonna ?" He kissed her lightly and was gone.

Lucrezia stood on the little balcony watching his strong figure as he strode along. How noble he was ! It was enough to have his love, even though the world had tried to break her heart. Yes ; she would always be happy so long as she had him—her Filippo ;

she would never be discontented again, even
though time was so long in passing when he
was away.   She smiled through her tears and
went to Filippino.   He had the same dark,
dreamy eyes and mirthful lips; the same
merry ways that she first loved in Filippo.

Fra Diamante, who was still painting with
Lippi at the Cathedral, sometimes stopped at
the door as he passed, to see if he could be of
any assistance in his master's absence.   One
afternoon Lucrezia had called him in to give
him some message from Filippo, when a figure
darkened the doorway, and looking up she
saw the proud, cold features of her cousin
Beatrice.   Lucrezia started, and paled a little.
Fra Diamante stepped back, then bowed to
Lucrezia, and left the house.   Beatrice smiled
a little disdainfully, and Lucrezia felt that
the visit boded her no good.

"Filippo is away?" she abruptly said, seat-
ing herself.   Lucrezia flushed a little under
the steady look, and stammered like a guilty
girl.

"But you are well cared for in his absence,"
she added suspiciously.   The flush died from

Lucrezia's face as she began to realize the imputation in Beatrice's undertone.

"I have word to you from your father," she continued, "he will receive you, if you will come back and never see——"

Lucrezia's eyes burned bright; she rose and interrupted Beatrice: "If that is what you have to tell me, you may go."

Beatrice walked languidly toward the door; there was an unconcealed look of hatred in her dark eyes. "Your father will be honored by the way his daughter receives his message," and she disdainfully left the room.

"It was not the message," sobbed Lucrezia to herself; "it was the messenger." If my father only knew Beatrice's motive; but it was long before I understood her—indeed, I do not know why she hates me so. I am sure it is she who has influenced my father against Filippo. She shall not separate us! How she looked at me that day she came to the convent; yet she was so loving; I trembled! And when she came before, in Florence, with that message from my father—ah! she means some harm to me! My cousin is cruel; she is a wicked woman," Lucrezia fiercely cried. "May the blessed Mother protect me—protect my Filippo!" she said, kneeling at the feet of the Virgin.

The Princess Beatrice, tall and straight, walked proudly down the street.

" My little cousin is showing great airs—she looked quite tragic; indeed, I really forgot my most important errand. Filippo is away, but where ? That was a handsome face under the cowl—but how he frowned at me ! Most men smile. Perhaps he will some time. I know him—Fra Diamante—I have seen him with Filippo ; now he is playing the part of the good pupil in his master's absence. How my little Lucrezia flushed! I entered at the right moment. She was looking up into his face, and there was an expression in his eyes a man always gives the woman he loves. Poof ! she resented my surmise—innocency ! I may as well visit the Countess Barbarina a little longer ; I can give my attention to my fair cousin in Filippo's absence. It will be quite worth my while, I fancy.

"She seems to win monks' hearts easily. I suppose golden hair attracts those dark, solemn men ; and Fra Diamante, I shall not forget the glance he gave me ; but he walked out of the room with the air of a prince. We will see how long Filippo thinks Lucrezia a saint. He must have loved her—men are such fools— or he would have tired of her long ago—the way he did with the rest of us. Strange I should care for him—a mere painter monk,—when a smile brings dukes and princes to my feet. . . . I remember the very first night he saw her—yet I did not realize the depth of it all at that time, I was so sure of his love. It was at the Grand Duke's palace, and Lucrezia came in the room dressed in that long, plain, robe-like gown—not a jewel, not a flower. Filippo was talking with me. I remember how he started and looked at her—but she was a child to me. . . .

"After all these months of labor with my uncle, to induce him to open his doors to her if she would leave Filippo, to be scorned as she scorned me this afternoon ! . . . I wonder

12

if I would give up my palace, and servants, and jewels to live in a little house with him ! Yes, it is love, but not a love like mine.   She is too ignorant of the world, but she is gaining in experience, I fancy. . . .

"Ah, Filippo! Filippo! you have evaded me, but I can now tell you things you may not like to hear.   I will accomplish it !" she exclaimed, "or I will separate them another way."

The color came and went in the cheeks of the Princess, as, with these thoughts, she walked from Lucrezia's house to the Countess Barbarina's.

Fra Diamante had hidden in the shadow until he saw her leave Lucrezia, then he followed a little distance behind.   "I know you well, my Princess," he thought, "but if eyes can watch, you will not bring harm to Lucrezia.   I think, too, that Fra Lippi is not in danger of your wiles.   You had better go back to Florence and your cavaliers there.   I wonder what she said to Lucrezia.   I saw what her eyes meant.   Poor child !   It would have been better if you had stayed in the convent of Santa Margharita."

XVI.

LUCREZIA longed for the days to go, it was so desolate without Filippo's smile. The Princess' visit had left its sting in her heart. She had come before in Florence with the same message to Lucrezia. Her father would welcome her to his home—her—but Filippino and Filippo—Beatrice must know she would never leave them. Her father knew that she would never come home under those circumstances. If he had only come to her instead of sending Beatrice, she knew that it would have been different. He was proud, but not harsh. He had wished her married to Senor Aletri, but he had never commanded it. She

179

knew that Beatrice was responsible for the estrangement. She should be so happy if it were not so. She had seen her father only once, since she bade him good-bye when she entered the convent ; that was one day when she was standing by the new palace Senor Pitti was building, and he went by. He had lost none of that imperious grace ; his face was still exceedingly handsome ; but it pained her to remember how thin and haggard he had grown. She had longed to cry out.

If he would come to see her—if he would talk with her but once—if Beatrice would be sincere !

Lucrezia grew pale and worn. The mid-summer sun beat down upon the steps and stones till the very air quivered with heat. The streets were so sun-baked, the trees so dusty and stunted,—how miserable it all was ! Filippo was yet in Perugia.

She looked towards the convent, hidden among olive and fruit-trees' foliage ; how cool the hill-side looked. How long ago it seemed since she leaned over the parapet and watched

the sunset light fade that night; how inde-
scribably perfect it was! How slowly the
moon rose. How long it was before the mid-
night-bell stroke. How the red roses burned
in the moonlight, as she stole down the path
to meet her lover; a dreamy look came into
her eyes, and a half smile trembled upon her
lips—long ago, was it? Why she could remember every detail of that night: how she
started when an orange dropped from its
stem, how she listened to her own heart-beat,
how she looked once back at the chapel door,
and wondered if the Abbess would allow the
portrait Madonna to stay in the chapel where
the nuns could see it. How she heard the
horses impatiently stepping up and down, a
little distance below; then she—oh, so carefully—slipped the bolt and swung back the
gate, to be caught in Filippo's arms. A
shadow fell across the steps, and a voice
cheerily sounded:

"Ah, Lucrezia *mia*, one would think it
midnight, moonlight, instead of mid-day and
scorching sun, by the half-awake dreams in

your eyes," and he lightly lifted himself by the iron rail to the low balcony where Lucrezia stood, and took her in his arms, kissing her smiling lips.

The glad light came into her eyes. "Oh, Filippo," she said, hiding her head in his bosom, "it has been so desolate since you went away!"

"*Cara mia*," he said, holding her off and looking into her face searchingly, "the red is in your cheeks now, but it looks as if it were but a sudden guest, and likely to leave as abruptly as it came. Lucrezia," he said tenderly, "I can see the blue veins in your hand, there are tears in your eyes; have you missed me so much, Lucrezia? Where is the *bambino*?" he suddenly exclaimed.

"He begged to go to the Cathedral with Fra Diamante; he was very much interested in Salome's dancing."

"Oh," laughed Filippo, "is the painting still going on with satisfaction to him—and Diamante?"

Lucrezia brought Lippi some bread and

wine, and they sat talking until the afternoon was almost gone, and Diamante stood in the door carrying Filippino on his shoulder.

The smiles and songs came back to Lucrezia's lips. The radiant gleam of Filippo's teeth, and the laughter of his beautiful dark eyes, made sunshine in the darkest corner of the little house. Ah! the sunny, flashing smile of Italy. But one day he came home with a look of melancholy as intense as the joyousness of his happiness. A deeper darkness came into his eyes as he met Lucrezia. Her smile died on her lips.

"Filippo!" she cried. What could have happened? it must be something horrible, for he was never sad at heart. The pain in his face deepened as he looked at her, and he sadly turned away, saying:

"Nothing, Lucrezia." He could not tell her that he had met a tall dark woman, whom he used to know in Florence,—her cousin—he could not tell her that she had waited at the Cathedral entrance until the workmen had gone home and he come out; he could not tell her that she caught his wrist to stay him, and in a very whirlwind of passion had tried to sear his soul with her story of Lucrezia's unfaithfulness and Fra Diamante's baseness; he could not tell her that he flung away this woman as if she had been a viper,—but her words had burned themselves into his heart in spite of all his love and trust.

Fra Diamante had not told Lucrezia that he had seen Beatrice still in Prato, yet with woman's intuition she someway knew that the trouble had come about through her cousin. She had not told Filippo of her cousin's visit in his absence, fearing to pain him; it always made him sad when her father's messages came. Her heart sank, but with a look of calm trust in her eyes she went to Filippo.

" Is it Beatrice ? " she asked.

Ah, if he could blot out those years; if he could take Lucrezia to his heart, with no memory of love words and caresses given to any other, his sweet-souled beloved ! If he had never known the Princess Beatrice ; Lucrezia

misunderstood the reason of his sadness, and
thought he had been told some false tale, yet
she knew he would never believe it. " Beatrice came here while you were in Perugia,"
she faltered ; she would say nothing about
the message, yet she must ; " my father
wished her to come ; I would not listen to
her. Fra Diamante was here, but left abruptly when she came,—and she went away
very angry. I have never seen her eyes look
so cruel. I was so nervous and frightened
until you came home ; oh ! " she cried, " I am
sure she would break my heart if she could ! "

Filippo drew Lucrezia close to his breast ;
she did not suspect, she did not question the
reason of her cousin's hatred, and he could
never tell her ; she must never know, not that
she would love him less or trust him less, but
it would sadden her.

" We will never think of her, *cara mia ;*
your pure soul cannot comprehend such a
woman."

His sweet Lucrezia ! he would always shelter
her from the cruelty of the world !

XVII.

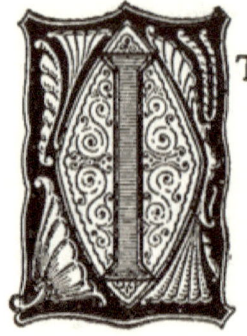IT was the sweet spring-tide! The meadows around Florence were white with great lilies. The hill-sides were not less snowy with the clusters of anemone. The peach-trees were rosy with buds. The cool ivy climbed about the stone. The green corn was springing from the sod. The grasses were bright with the color of wild tulips and poppies. The violets were blossoming, the air was full of dreamy fragrance. The birds sang in the groves ; the lizards darted in and out, rustling the dead leaves ; the warm breezes brought the hum of insects ; the sunshine was soft, yet radiant.

All Italy had awakened and smiled as if her sleep were but one long love-dream.

"Let us forth, Lucrezia *mia*," said Filippo, leaning to kiss her on the brow, as he camé softly into her little apartment and found her seated near the window, seeming to watch the fleecy clouds flitting across the blue sky, though the tears which filled her eyes betrayed that her thoughts were elsewhere.

"Let us forth, and if our parting cannot be joyous, our sadness the last day will not be increased if we linger away some of the moments where we have spent so many sweetest hours!"

He lifted her chin upward as he stood behind bending over her, and kissed the tears away, then folding her in his arms, continued :

"Come, and it shall be a happy day with us! The memory of all we are to each other, coming over us anew, will make us strong for this separation, the longest, *carina mia*, that we have known in these short ten years. The hope of return, the trust in our mutual love,— what comforts are these, Lucrezia! Come, and Filippino shall go with us. Even now he is gleefully waiting for us ; I told him as I came from the court. Come, and we shall dry these tears."

He stroked her hair gently. Lucrezia arose and threw her arms about his neck. Her speech was a caress.

They descended the stone staircase to the groined entrance court, where Filippino ran laughingly to grasp his mother's hand. The grim outer doors with the scrolled hinges admitted them to the street, and they were soon threading the gayly peopled Piazza della Signoria, interrupted occasionally in their lovers' talk by the passing salutation of acquaintances. Filippino, running a short distance before them, returned now and then for a smile, or a *crazia* to drop into an old *poverino's* hat.

It was one of those days when the Italian yields himself with special freedom to the delight of the season.

The equipage of the Grand Duke passed rapidly through the Piazza. The flower girl,

Spoleto.

nodding and smiling, distributed her violets embedded in geranium, with a *buona festa* for as many as noticed her. The blind beggar touched his harp, while a boy at his side accompanied the monotonous strains with the constant *dartem qualchecosa.*

People were moving to and fro, or talking in stationary groups. Once or twice a friend, knowing the departure for Spoleto on the morrow, left those with whom he was talking or walking and accompanied Lippi and Lucrezia a little space, and then, with a *buona sera,* tenderly uttered in delicate sympathy for the separation, glided away from the loving pair.

Hardly conscious of the streets through which they passed, they reached the Ponte S. Trinita, pausing to lean upon the parapet and look down upon the smooth waters of the Arno, the ripple almost inaudible. Filippino, finding a stone much heavier than he could lift, rolled it down from the height into the river, laughing merrily at the great splash that followed. Another stone was rolled through the same opening in the bridge. The child called a second time to his parents to look, and wondered why they smiled so faintly.

" And you think it may be several months before the apse is painted ? " continued Lucrezia.

" There is so much to do, but I shall hasten the work as much as possible, my Lucrezia. The Commune has engaged me for more than the Holy Virgin."

" It is the longest distance we have ever been apart !—and Perugia seemed so far."

" I know it, dear one ! Would that I might hold you ever to my heart, and never leave my beloved !"

They continued their walk, and reaching the limits of the city, came upon a quiet road walled on one side and overlooking on the other a broad valley covered with olive trees and containing several villas and small dwellings. They were soothed by the gentle landscape, and coming upon a fantastic bench made of branches, seated themselves, Filippino meanwhile amused himself in gathering violets and anemones from the hill-side to bring them.

"Filippo," said Lucrezia, "it is only what
you will be able to do at Spoleto that, with
the blessing of the Holy Mother, helps me to
bear this separation. If you could but know
how happy I am in the knowledge of the
praises that are being poured upon you. And
Lucrezia is a woman, not a child! Though
every hour shall seem twice—thrice—its natural
length, I shall try to await patiently your return. Yet always it will be so hard!"

"Always, my thoughts will be of her I love,"
replied Lippi, tenderly. "Remember," and he
drew her attention to a road in the plain below
that led in the direction of Prato, "remember
you, my love, that early morning when we first
came to Florence?" and he smiled, as he knew
how to both it was as yesterday. Ten years
ago! Eh! these days that go all too fast!
"Beloved,"—and he drew her closer to him
with his arm about her,—"before I knew you
I knew not myself. I loved the wild whirl of
passion—that which had no bounds. Only of
myself I thought—the enjoyment of the hour.
With you, how changed this world. Happy

the day—the hour when at Santa Margharita's
I knew your love! Think you," and he kissed
her as he smiled, "think you the Pope's dis-
pensation will make you more mine own?
No! no!"

"And never for one moment would you
listen to what Beatrice——"

"Speak not of her," said Lippi quickly,
"know you not, my heart's love, the trust
which I have ever had in you? *Dio!*" and he
spoke with flashing eyes, "how I loathe her!
hate her! how the very thought of her stings
me to the heart's core. Never, never, would
I have believed her treacherous!"

He would have continued, but Filippino
came running towards them, his hands full of
flowers. "See! see!" he cried gleefully, and
threw them into his mother's lap as he scampered away for more.

"It is the color that he loves so," Lippi said
fondly, as they watched the child upon the
hill-side. He, too, will be a painter. Each
day he surprises me yet the more. He
will be greater than his father," and Lippi

laughed heartily; "he must have what I lack, and he inherits that from his mother's nature. Lucrezia, this is a dawn of a wonderful spirit —we shall live to see great painters. There is a youth in Perugia, a gentle lad like Filippino, who loved to stand and gaze while I painted, and he would copy as I drew. One day I gave him the brush and colors to use, and my eyes could hardly believe the luminous color and sentimental grace of the little picture he made. Then there is Tommasio's son, who makes dainty fragments into all manner of delicate garlands for gay ladies—they already call him Ghirlandajo. It is a picture to see him in his dark shop, piercing and twisting the gold and silver filagree, and great ladies in their sweeping gowns and exquisite laces and jewels patting his round cheeks and praising him. But Filippino,"—and they fell to building the little air castles for the future.

"Diamante will doubtless remain with me during my stay at Spoleto," said Lippi when they had resumed the subject of the journey and frescoing; "I do not know what I should

13

do without his help.　There is no one to whom
I would trust so much.　Often I have thought
there should be no other teacher for Filippino,
if by any chance—" he stopped and smiled
brightly as he saw Lucrezia's pained look.

"Speak not of any chance," she said, almost
trembling, as she held Filippo's arm more
closely.

"No chance, then, my little one," said Lippi
soothingly, and though there was some mirth
in his smile, there was tenderness, pathos, in
its depths.　"Always shall I be with you;
Spoleto days will go."　They sat talking till
the shadows had grown much longer.

"And as often as possible you will send me
messages?" asked Lucrezia.

"Yes, *carina mia !*　And now," he said, calling Filippino to him, who came proudly bearing aloft a branch of peach blossoms which he
gave to his father, "let us move homeward.
There are several matters which need my
attention before I leave the city, and the
afternoon is waning.　But I could stay here
forever with you, my sweet, true love."

Madonna and Child.
Fra Lippo Lippi.

"Yes, we must go," replied Lucrezia.

They left the peaceful road and mingled again in the city's din, never to forget the memory of the happy hours.

After the evening meal was over, when the sunset light began to fade, Lippi took Lucrezia by the hand and gently drew her to the window seat. Over the whole Val d'Arno a faint transparent mist arose. The magnolia shone white. The sighing of the wind through the leafy bowers made dream-like music. The dying light touched the room with tender hues then faded away. Now and then the lighted torches gleamed, then the city grew silvery in the moonlight.

"But thy dear face is ever before me," murmured Lippi, "and it is with my heart full of love that I paint you for the Virgin. Those years before I saw you, love! I wondered that I made a Virgin worth worshipping. Oh, those blessed days in the convent! remember, then your own dear self was near—I could look into your eyes and see your smile; you were then the bride, *carina*, and know

you what added dignity and grace has come
to you since?   It is marvellously sweet and
beautiful!   There, love, one moment—do not
move.   That is the way I shall paint you for
L'Incoronata, at Spoleto,—your eyes meekly
cast down, your fair head bent as if to receive
a coronet—the sorrow and suffering past."

"They are," she smiled,

"You are an image of some bright eternity!
You shall be clad in regal robes—in pictures
you know I can so dress you,—a white robe
embroidered with golden suns.   The court of
heaven will be peopled with glorified spirits;
the canonized fathers and doctors will be looking at you admiring—there will be some of the
suitors whose rod did not blossom.—Shall I
paint Guido Aletri's face as——"

"Oh, hush!" she cried, putting her hand
over his mouth.   A fitful look of melancholy
came to his face.

"*Carina*, if Senor Aletri had been a successful suitor, then indeed you would have been in
the midst of a court. Do you never regret——"
But his sentence was not finished.   Lucrezia

drew his head to her breast and smothered his words in kisses. " You loved me from the very first, dear one ? Ah ! Lucrezia *mia*, what grace was there in me that you should leave all and come to me ? Is love indeed blind ?"

" No, no," she protested, "love sees, it sees." He drew her to his heart.

" Mine, mine ! Oh, if I could give these features to the world as my heart sees them— my perfect type of maidenhood and mother- hood !

> "' Virgine Madre, figlia del tuo figlio,
> Umile ed alta piu che creatura,
> Termine fisso d'eterno consiglio,'"

he softly repeated.

The first glimmering of dawn found Fra Lippi and Fra Diamante prepared for their journey. A last *addio* and yet another was given to one who looked down tearfully from her casement, starting at the sound of horses' hoofs along the deserted streets, and as they died away, breathing a prayer for the safe re- turn of her beloved.

XVIII.

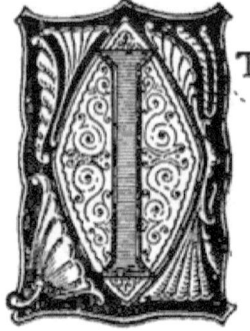T was a three days' journey to Spoleto.

The route was by way of Perugia. Following the road from the Porta di San Nicolo, Lippi and Diamante crossed the range of hills which separated the Val d'Arno from the Val d'Arno di Sopra.

Never was the view from the summit of the pass of San Donato more beautiful than on that morning, when looking back over the valley of Florence, they could see clearly the snow-capped mountains of the Lucchese and Modenese Apennines.

Turning the horses and resuming the journey, after the long gaze, the lovely upper Val

198

d'Arno lay stretched out before them, and in the distance rose the mountains of La Falerino and Casentino.

The noon-day found the travellers at San Giovanni. " While the horses rest," said Lippi, as he sat opposite Diamante at the table of the inn, where they had refreshed themselves after the long ride in the appetizing air, "we may spend the hour at San Lorenzo. How little the country folk here knew what would become of their '*shift-less wool-gatherer.*' Remember, Diamante, what Fra Anselmo told us at the Carmine of Tommaso Guido's boyhood here ? Their *Masaccio !* 'Lubberly Tom,' as the people called him. Ha! ha! how the name went with him to the Brancacci Chapel ! "

" Yes," said Diamante, as he replaced the wineglass on the table, and Lippi filled it again, "you remember the day the master found you there and praised the coloring ?"

"Remember! that I do !" replied Lippi earnestly, "and what he said, as if it were but yesterday. I can see him now, entering the chapel and coming towards me. Some poor wool-gatherer, I thought, who would say his prayers. His garments were so old, so ill-fitting. I had always pictured the master differently; but it was his genius that made him forget himself, neglect himself, until all laughed at him, to their shame! Engrossed in his ideals, he wandered alone, contented with his thoughts as his best companions."

"How often we have heard of his great, generous heart eager to encourage," said Diamante.

"It was so that day in the chapel!" exclaimed Lippi. "Looking up from my painting, he was standing beside me. 'That is right, my boy!' he said; 'Masaccio has heard of you.' At the words my hand trembled. *Masaccio!* My brush would have fallen! Was this he? Never had I known such fear to paint in the presence of another. 'No, no, boy!' he cried. 'It is only Masaccio!' and forthwith he took the palette from my hand and praised my Virgin's face, touching it here and there till it glowed with life. 'Yes, you

shall paint wonderfully!' he said. 'This is
the true spirit! Paint the men and women
about you, boy,—real flesh and blood.' How
I could have fallen upon my knees before him
—him whom I had always worshipped! Never
did I see him again. The pity of it!"
Lippi's face darkened. " The pity of it, that
he, the only one,—Diamante,—the only true
painter, should have died in such a way—
poisoned! Curses on them who did it!
Curses!" Fra Lippi's great eyes flashed.

The two men rose from the table, and passing into the street, walked to the chapel of
San Lorenzo, where before Masaccio's Virgin
and Child, on the right of the high altar, they
talked tenderly and earnestly of the great
master.

This was still the topic of the afternoon,
when, having returned to the inn and mounted
their horses, they journeyed to Arezzo, where,
arriving at twilight, the first night was spent.

"Never do I think of Arezzo," said Lippi
to Diamante, as next morning they continued
their journey, passing along the plain, " but

my heart goes to Lucrezia. How I tried again and again for the ideal face in painting the *L'Incoronata* for Carlo Marzuppini for the chapel of San Bernado. I had not seen my love then ! How different when only a few months ago I painted the Virgin at San Domenico in Perugia. We shall be there to-night."

The third and last day of the journey led from Perugia to San Maria degli Angeli to Foligno, to Le Vene, and as the setting sun touched the horizon, Spoleto with its towers, castles, and forest background came in sight.

As the travellers drew nearer they could discern the old fortress and its vast aqueduct. There, too, was the great ravine, dark with shadows, while the hill-sides were tinted with the light of the dying day and the clouds aglow with the glory of the setting sun.

" Yes, this will be our home until the summer be wellnigh past," said Diamante, as they quickened their horses in the gathering darkness.

" Let us trust no longer," exclaimed Lippi. " My heart is far back in Florence. These

weeks! These months! Too long! I am
lonely to-night!"

A look of melancholy shadowed Diamante's
face, but its secret was known only to himself, and never yet, and never should be—by
the mercy of the Virgin—betrayed.

With a smile he turned to Lippi, and spoke
cheering words.

The next morning found the painters in the
Cathedral, marking out the spaces in the choir
for the frescos.

The work of the Cathedral progressed
slowly. Days passed into weeks. There was
but little variety in each day's task. The
painters left their lodgings at early morning,
and, save for the brief interval for refreshment
at noon-day, continued eagerly at work until
the gathering darkness at sunset forbade.
More than once Lippi was at Santa Maria
Assunta at dawn, before there was light sufficient to see the walls—so impatient was he to
hasten the frescoing.

"I awoke!" he would explain when Diamante came to call him to the morning

meal. "I could not sleep again. There is so much yet to do. After the Annunciation and the Nativity, the Death of the Virgin and the Coronation. Then to Florence!"

The members of the Commune visited the Cathedral from time to time, to approve and suggest. There were always delays, it seemed to the impatient soul of Fra Lippi.

"But it will all be finished some time, dear one!" he would exclaim again and again in the love messages to Lucrezia. "With Filippino, do you watch as eagerly for my coming as I here await the time of my going to you? Ah! this parting! My heart's love! It must never be so again! The image of your dear face blesses me day by day, or how else could I paint? Thou beloved inspirer of my Madonnas!"

Frequently, when the shadows began to fill the church at twilight, Lippi and Diamante would stroll through the town to the Porta d'Annibale, or, ascending to the citadel, watch from the castle walls the darkness slowly settling down over the valley of the Clitum-

Santa Maria Assunta (Spoleto)

nus. Often, too, following the road outside the town, they passed beyond the aqueduct to the Monte Luco, with its monastery of San Guiliano and grove of oaks.

At last all was finished but the Coronation. "Only a little longer!" joyously exclaimed Lippi to Diamante as they returned one night in the moonlight from Monte Luco, and, having entered the town, were in the street leading to the Piazza of Santa Maria Assunta.

The night was radiant—sky and houses and people aglow with silvery beams. Merry groups were passing to and fro in the streets. There was music, singing, happiness—all the gentleness of a perfect night. The monks walked more slowly in the moonlight.

Suddenly a face—Lippi started. A woman, unattended, looked up into his face in passing. It was only a moment's meeting. He looked back—she had disappeared in the throng.

But that face! The memories were horrible to him. Why was she here? Could it be his eyes had deceived him? Impossible! He could never mistake. He faltered—

stopped—recovered himself. *Eh!* But Diamante had not seen, nor should he know.

" Let us hasten," he said, taking Diamante's
arm.

At dawn the next morning Lippi had come
to the Cathedral alone. He could not sleep.

" Strange that seeing her should have kept
me awake through the long night. She seeks
me surely. But, Beatrice, it is all in vain.
Think you here in Spoleto I have forgotten
my Lucrezia? No! no!"

He crossed the chancel to a table near the
altar, and, pouring wine from the flagon,
drank. Replacing the cup, he ascended the
staging to the Coronation. A half hour of
stillness in the great church; suddenly an
open door—a woman glided to the chancel.

" Filippo!"

He knew her voice.

" Filippo!"

Now he knew what was in that voice—
resolution, passion, desperation.

"Filippo! Listen!" He looked down upon
the upturned face—the pale cheeks, the trem-

bling, white lips, the fierce, burning, deep-set
eyes. Where was the color, the warmth, the
radiance of the Princess Beatrice? Had she
changed so much? Ah, the look!

"You saw me last night! You knew me!"
The husky voice became almost a hiss. "I
have watched your every movement. You
cannot evade me—I follow you!"

"Leave me!" and Lippi's voice trembled
with anger. "Why come you hither? Know
you not what I have told you? It is no use.
Leave me, I say! Leave me!"

"Never! Never! I follow you forever!
Oh, Filippo, is it all in vain? Dare you tell
me so? You dare not!"

A darker look came into her face; she
stepped to the table near the altar.

"Have I not told you again and again?"
cried Lippi. I will not listen to you! I
loathe you!"

He turned to the wall to paint.

The woman leaned heavily against the table,
then bent over it a moment—but Filippo did
not even turn to look. There was a moment's

silence, retreating footsteps—the opening of
the Cathedral door,—she paused, half lifted
her arms in entreaty,—but Lippi was painting
the robe of the Virgin, whose face was Lucrezia's, looking down upon her—the door closed,
and she was gone.

Lippi felt that a demon had been there.
There was no softness, nor even pity, in his
heart for the wretched woman who loved him.

A curse upon her!   How unsteady his hand
was !   At this rate the picture would never be
finished.—His blessed Lucrezia,—her   soft
glance and sweet smile seemed resting upon
him.

He would walk a moment, till he should forget the other.   He descended the staging,
and lifted the wine-glass to his lips.

XIX.

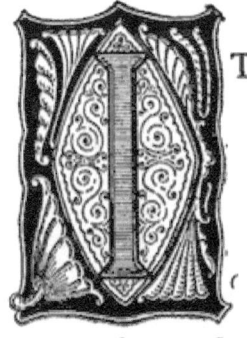T was the second week of October. In the heat of the Tuscan sun the grapes had ripened, the corn had been gathered, the violets and anemones had faded. Yet there were always flowers; the damask rose and the cyclamen were in blossom ; the fresh bloom of spring and the radiant loveliness of summer had changed to a beauty that still made Florence the fairest of the fair. The deeper blue of the sky, the clear air, the gleam of sunshine on painted fields, forests, and hillsides, joined to make more beautiful autumn's great fresco. Though the *contadini* had cut the hay and pressed their grapes, though the

mountains were bronze and scarlet, though there were cool shadows in the gorges, there was no foreboding of winter in the air. Italy smiled in the one love-life.

Sure, the ice-laden winds from the Apennines would blow bitterly down the Arno. But what if winter were coming ! Why the to-morrow, when to-day lengthened the beauteous past, and brought the sweet springtide one day nearer !

That morning Lucrezia stood on the little balcony and breathed more happiness to her soul ;—Filippo was coming !

Higher ! not content whence she could look down only the narrow street. Higher ! since she might see far away, beyond the Arno, flowing full below, reflecting *loggias*, balconies, palaces ; beyond bridges, cupolas, spires ; beyond the great Duomo dome, to the mountains,—for he was coming ! The second week in October ! That was the message. How long the weeks had been, but she would forget it all in the sunshine of his smile ! He would soon be with her. Oh ! the long

journey—a hundred miles! Would he stop
at Perugia? No! no! He would hasten,
she knew. And he did love her. She
laughed a little, yet weeping too. She was
so happy! Filippino ran into the porch to
play, and, looking up, saw her. He held out
a little picture towards her. She hastened
down to catch him to her heart, and kiss
his curling hair.

"Yes, dear! that is wonderful," she said.
"You will one day paint great pictures with
your father!" He ran off gleefully to play.
Lucrezia folded the paper and put it in her
breast, to keep to show to Filippo.

How much to her was this great love!
How lonely, miserable was life without her
beloved! How proud of him! And the
Commune at Spoleto sent for him because
of what Cosmo de Medici had said. To
think of the praises! Those beautiful frescos
at Prato; his St. Stephen and St. John!—
men stood before them and wept.

How glad she was that she had left the
convent for his love. This was more than

all else to her.   How tenderly he would kiss
her when he came, breathing those sweetest of words she knew so well; and she—she
would throw her arms about his neck and kiss
him again and again.   Oh, the wicked Beatrice! and, for the moment, the old dark
shadow fell upon Lucrezia's heart; but no!
no! he cannot, he does not believe!   He
loves me!

And again she was weeping in the little
balcony where she first stood.   She looked
down the street.   Why! there was a Carmelite monk!   The white mantle startled her.
Her heart gave a great leap.   A flood of
happiness poured into her soul.   Could it be
Filippo, was he coming earlier, to give her a
joyful surprise?   She waited breathlessly, for
she could not distinguish the face.

A great disappointment began to steal over
her.   No! it was not her dear one.   That
was not his figure, that was not his gait.   But
ah! no!—yes! it was Diamante!   Why was
he alone?   A thousand thoughts rushed into
her mind.   Perhaps there had been delay

in the work at Santa Maria Assunta—and she remembered what Filippo told her about the great semidome of the apse, not simply Christ crowning the Virgin,—but he was to paint angels, and sibyls, and prophets. That was it! He had not accomplished as much as he expected, and he must stay a little longer. And he had sent Diamante before him to tell her not to be disappointed,—not to be anxious,—for he was coming. He was working as fast as possible—he was so eager to be with her.

How good and kind and thoughtful he was, always! If he only need not go back again!— but the rectors wished him to paint so many pictures. But soon he was coming—coming to rest a little first. She would try not to be disappointed now ; she would force back the tears and be happy.

She stood ready to nod and smile when Diamante looked towards her. And now he was only a few houses away. Yes ! he was looking. But, oh ! why does he stride along so solemnly with downcast eyes and no smile

in answer to her salutation—he, who was
always so merry?   What can it mean?

Eh, Dio! what a dark look was in his face!
What can have happened?   And why did he
not speak, now that he was so near?   A great
horror came over Lucrezia.   She stood motionless, speechless, looking at Diamante.   But
suddenly turning, she rushed from the balcony
through the house, to meet him as he entered.

"Tell me! oh, tell me!" she cried, white
and trembling, grasping his arm.   "Filippo?
Has any thing happened?   Why are you
alone? is he ill?   I must go to him!"

But she could question no more.   Diamante struggled with his emotion.   He gently
unclasped her hand from his arm, and taking
it in his, led her tenderly to the window seat,
the favorite of her beloved.

"Be brave, Lucrezia," he said sadly, looking down into her upturned face, so eagerly
fixed upon him; "a great sorrow has come to
you.   I cannot tell you gently!   I must not
keep back the truth"—and his voice wavered
and grew husky—"Oh! may the Blessed

Mother comfort you! Filippo — Filippo — is dead!"

With a great sob her head sank upon her bosom. She clasped her hands to her face.

"O Santa Maria de Misericordia!" she cried; "Santa Maria de Misericordia!"

How dark, how drear, how weary the world is after all!

"I will not cry or even weep while you tell me," she said piteously, looking up at last. For a moment, she again hid her face in her hands. "I must know!" and she bravely tried to keep back her grief, yet great tears rolled down from her beautiful eyes. "I must know!—O my Filippo!"

"There is little to tell," said Diamante, turning towards her from the window, to which he had gone and was looking far away, a great sorrow and pity upon his face.

"Yesterday morning he did not come to Santa Maria Assunta. I sought him; I found him very ill,—he did not know me. Again and again he called for his beloved. He thought you were with him at the last.

Lucrezia, was his last word.   Then——" but Fra Diamante could say no more.

Ah! poor Lucrezia! poor little girl!

There would be no noon to her sweet dawn, only night, dark, silent midnight.

Filippo! Filippo!

The sun would shine, but its brightness would be dim.   Summer clouds would spread over the sky, but they would be heavy and black.   The seasons would come and go, the hill-sides would smile with flowers, the fruit would hang heavy on its vines and boughs, the nightingale's note would be heard, the white and scarlet and purple lilies would blossom around Florence, the snow-peaks of the mountains would glow and pale in the sunset light in the shade of the ilex tree, the lucciola would gleam, the youths and maidens would laugh in their joy—but the dear presence of her beloved was forever taken from her.

Only in dreams would she see the love-light shining in his eyes and the radiant smile upon his lips.   *Dio Mio!*   Only in memory would she hear the tender music of his voice!

Alone in the still, dark church! The eyes closed, the voice silent, the hands upon his breast! But ah, God! the smile must yet be upon his lips!

Filippo! Filippo!

He was with the saints he had shown to men. He was now looking upon the loving face of the Most Merciful Madre,—the face he had labored so earnestly, so carefully, to paint on earth.

XX

UT Fra Diamante had not told Lucrezia all. A horrid suspicion, burning deeper and deeper during the hours of the long journey to her, as he spurred the horse onward from Spoleto, filled his whole soul with fury.

But not now should Lucrezia know. Her grief was too much even for the present. He would not even hint that there was treachery, that one of her own family could do so foul a deed. He would not tell her how, yesterday morning, on his way to Lippi, he met a woman —dark, low-browed, and stately ; how, after death had come, he saw her again, standing in the shadow of Santa Maria Assunta ; how, in

the passion with which his soul was beginning
to be charged, he rushed towards her, grasping
her hands, crying :

" Woman !"

" Let me go.   Why hold me thus ?"

" Woman, think you I did not know.   You
did it;   Curses on you !"

" Mad-monk, you lie !"   Let me free, I say !
Let me go !"   And wrenching herself from
his grasp, pushing him back with the fury of a
tigress, Beatrice was gone.   Guilt and terror
were stamped upon her face.

Vengeance !   Is there no justice ?   Vengeance !

But Beatrice and her power !

The great, cold, evil world !   Would it believe ?   He himself knew the threats, the hate,
the awful bitterness with which the dead man's
steps were dogged.   And now there was poison
in the wine !

But God would avenge ; was not vengeance
His ?

XXI.

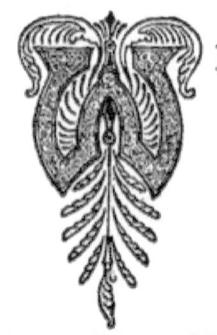INTER was indeed coming. Winter—so drear, so drear! The new-fallen snow was upon the mountains. The sky was steel-hued, the country bare, desolate ; the north wind sullen. The old sweet Tuscan life was gone. The bells rang as if a wail for the dead.

Ah, Fiorenza, never a laugh without its sigh ! Never a song without tears !

Winter was there. Many a night mother and child sobbed themselves to sleep in each other's arms.

After Diamante's return from Spoleto, where he had gone to finish the fresco, Lucrezia gave Filippino into his care.

"Take him," she said, coming to him one morning, "it was his father's wish."

They were in the Church of Santa Maria Primerana, and looked up at the *Annunciation* of her Filippo. "For his sake!" said Diamante. In his heart he added: "And for her sake!"

Brave and strong, yet Lucrezia found no comfort. In vain Lorenzo de Medici came to her with praises for her beloved. In vain the long journey to the Holy Father, that he might give his absolution and his blessing. These could help, but not heal. To stand beside the marble tomb, erected near the altar of the Cathedral where last her beloved worked, by one who had honored and loved him—that was, in its way, a solace; to visit his paintings, to kneel before them as at some sacred shrine; to look up at his last Madonna—but he was not there!

She had come back to the convent of Santa Margharita—there could be no other shelter so sweet. She opened the chapel door; the altar and shrine were veiled and draped in rich violet hue—the mourning color which tells of the approach of Holy Week. Through the open door she heard the nuns chanting the Miserere.

She stood outside the chancel. The curtains of the canopy of the altar were drawn aside, and on a cross before her was the slain Christ.

It was to the feet of Him she had come to lay down her burden. In the curtained arch she stood, calm and pale, her large, dark, intense eyes looking back upon the years gone by.

With a cry, she threw herself before the picture painted by the dear hand, and in the still church the Virgin looked down at her with tender sorrow, as if she would place her hand on the bowed head and promise comfort for the bruisèd heart.

XXII.

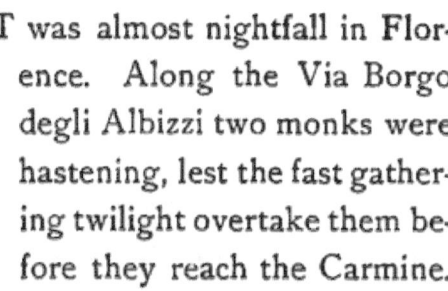T was almost nightfall in Florence. Along the Via Borgo degli Albizzi two monks were hastening, lest the fast gathering twilight overtake them before they reach the Carmine.

The older wore his cowl drawn far over his brow, and walked like a man oppressed by sorrows.

The youth had, in the haste of walking, half pushed back his cowl, and showed a delicate, handsome face framed by a mass of black waving hair. He was tall and dark and straight, and walked with buoyant step ; his eyes were large and lustrous, with dreamy lids ; his lips curved and sweet, and smiled as if the

cup of life—the rim of which they had hardly
more than touched—was full and sparkling, a
wellspring of joy and gladness, at whose bottom was no hint of bitter waters. He was
looking up at a balcony, where a woman in
trailing velvet and exquisite lace was standing
in the fading sunset light—some great person-
age in jewels and flowers ; there was a background of palms, the sound of music and
laughter, and as he drew nearer he could see
through the low open window gay ladies and
courtiers. The woman was smiling in the
face of a man in blue velvet and satin half
lying across the balustrade. She touched the
lute and began to sing. Suddenly she looked
down into the street. Her hand fell across
the lute-strings and made a strange, jarring
discord. The song died upon her lips.

White and trembling, she leaned over the
railing and looked into the young Carmelite's
eyes, as if a ghost had come again to haunt
her. The older monk glanced up. With a
mighty effort the woman drew herself back
and began the song, but a string snapped, the

lute fell upon the marble and broke; as the monks passed there was silence.

The youth turned to his companion, but the cowl was more about his face than before, and concealed the strained compression of the lips and the fierce light burning in his eyes.

"What a face!" the young monk cried. "It was as though she had looked upon heaven and hell! It is strangely familiar—ah! it is that head among my father's drawings—his Herodias!—I must some time paint it—after I finish the frescos in the Brancacci Chapel," and Filippino's thoughts went out into the Future.

But Fra Diamante drew his white mantle closer about him, and made no answer. He was of the Past, and his thoughts were with it.

THE END.